WAKING the DEAD

and other
FUN ACTIVITIES

CASEY LYALL

WAKING the DEAD

and other FUN ACTIVITIES

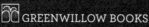 GREENWILLOW BOOKS

an Imprint of HarperCollins*Publishers*

Waking the Dead and Other Fun Activities
Copyright © 2024 by Casey Lyall

The text of this book is set in Iowan Old Style.
Book design by Sylvie Le Floc'h
Illustrations by Andy Smith

Library of Congress Cataloging-in-Publication Data

Names: Lyall, Casey, author.
Title: Waking the dead and other fun activities / by Casey Lyall.
Description: New York : Greenwillow Books, an Imprint of HarperCollins Publishers, 2024. | Audience: Ages 8-12. | Audience: Grades 4-6. | Summary: "Twelve-year-old Kimmy Jones discovers secrets about her heritage and learns about a witch who has been wreaking havoc for centuries"— Provided by publisher.
Identifiers: LCCN 2024001345 (print) | LCCN 2024001346 (ebook) | ISBN 9780063239876 (hardcover) | ISBN 9780063239890 (ebook)
Subjects: CYAC: Witches—Fiction. | Dead—Fiction. | Spirits—Fiction. | Mystery and detective stories. | LCGFT: Witch fiction. | Detective and -mystery fiction. | Novels.
Classification: LCC PZ7.1.L94 Wak 2024 (print) | LCC PZ7.1.L94 (ebook) | DDC [Fic]—dc23
LC record available at https://lccn.loc.gov/2024001345
LC ebook record available at https://lccn.loc.gov/2024001346
24 25 26 27 28 LBC 5 4 3 2 1
First Edition
Greenwillow Books

For my parents, Nicki and Tom

WAKING the DEAD

and other FUN ACTIVITIES

Chapter One

Bringing people back to life was an unusual service for a funeral home, but it was one my family did with great pride.

Unless the deceased in question was my grandmother's mortal enemy.

Apparently, then, we got a little cranky about it.

"I swear that woman died first just to beat me at something," Grandma Bev grumbled as we went down to the basement, where Alma Waters was waiting for us to prep her for her final rest. Starting with our special step.

Grandma headed to the table that held Alma and removed the sheet while I lowered the lights. Ambience was key. One of the first things I'd learned was how disorienting an experience Waking could be for someone. Having to squint through the bright fluorescent lights of the prep room on top of that? Not comforting.

After turning on the battery-powered tea candles, I settled in on a stool beside Grandma.

"Do you think she'll Wake?" I peered down at Alma's still form. Only those with unfinished business had a spark of life left hanging around for us to connect with. They were the ones who needed us the most.

The ones we offered a last wish to.

"You're the one in training, Kimmy," Grandma said with a little sideways smile. "Reach out with your power and you tell me."

Oh, right. I straightened in my seat.

After years of watching Grandma do this, I was still getting used to being allowed to Wake someone myself.

Every member of the Jones family was born with the ability, but training didn't begin until you turned twelve because *tradition*. According to Grandma, anyway. I had no way to fact-check her since we were the only two left on the family tree.

I'd turned twelve a couple of months ago in January and couldn't wait to dive right in. *Finally*, it was my turn to help.

It didn't take long for me to realize that learning how to harness the power was harder than it looked.

I took Alma's cool hand in mine. *Don't let go,* I reminded myself. There had to be a physical connection for the power to find the remaining spark. If you let go, the connection was lost and the person you Woke went back to rest. Abruptly.

It wasn't a pleasant sensation. Or so Mrs. Sims, the first person I ever Woke, told me after I accidentally did that to her. That was an awkward apology to make.

Hence the reminder.

As excited as I was, it was still sinking in how big a responsibility I was taking on.

This was the final moment in a person's life! Or was it the first moment of their death? Either way, sometimes I had doubts about placing it in the hands of a twelve-year-old. But every Jones before me had made it through training at this age and Grandma was sure I would, too.

"Kimmy," she murmured over my shoulder. "You know what to do. Trust yourself."

Easier said than done, but I nodded anyway.

"Start with your breathing," Grandma instructed.

I closed my eyes and began breathing in through my nose and out through my mouth. The first two weeks of my training had been strictly breathing. Not how I thought it was going to start, but Grandma said grounding yourself was the most important preparation for using our power. So, I breathed.

In.

And out.

"Find your center," she said. "And reach for the power."

As I focused inward, the warm vibration in the middle of my chest made me smile. Ever since the first time I'd managed to connect with it, that was how my power always felt.

Bright and welcoming.

Along the edges was the familiar presence of Grandma. When I first noticed it, she'd told me it was the thread of connection that passed the power down through our family. Spreading to us all, reaching out like the roots of a tree.

If my dad was alive, I'd be able to feel him, too.

"Visualize the path," Grandma continued. "Remember, you're in control."

Visualizing. Another one of Grandma's steps I thought was silly at first, but now—

Well, now it was as easy as breathing.

I pictured my power as a pulsing golden ball of light and then imagined the light spreading from my chest, down through my arms, and into Alma's hand.

Sweeping through her, searching until—

There. A tiny warm spot.

Her leftover spark.

"She's here," I said.

"Of course she is," Grandma replied. "Alma wouldn't leave without at least *trying* to get the last word in." She sighed and I cracked my eyes open to peek at her. "Go on, then."

"Um, Grandma?" I motioned to my face with my free hand, trying to hint about the scowl on hers.

"What?" She wiped at the side of her mouth and checked her thumb for lipstick. As if her coat of Parisian Red would dare smudge.

"You always say people should wake up to a friendly face," I reminded her as I poked the corners of my own mouth into a smile.

"Alma is very familiar with me looking at her like this," she said. "It'll be comforting." She waved off my concerns and nudged me forward. "Now for the spark," Grandma prompted me with the next step.

The most important one.

The spark, that small remaining piece of a life force drifting inside the recently deceased. Unable to do anything on its own, it would eventually move on—but a Jones could reach out and anchor it long enough to Wake the person and find out their last wish. Clearing up their unfinished business.

Closing my eyes again, I pictured the golden light of my power surrounding Alma's spark like a cocoon. Between one heartbeat and the next, everything clicked.

I anchored the spark. Alma took a breath.

Her eyelids fluttered and slowly opened. I grasped her hand tight before she could jerk it away, proud of myself for keeping steady as the deep thrum of the connection took hold.

"Hello, Mrs. Waters," I said quietly as she focused her gaze on us. "You're at the Jones Family Funeral Home. Unfortunately, you have passed away, but—"

"Bev," she croaked. "What kind of hokity-pokity stuff is your family into?"

"Hokity—" Grandma sputtered. "Our family has a special gift, *Alma*. One we're using to ensure that you can complete any unfinished business. Do you want to take us up on it, or should we send you back on your way?"

That definitely wasn't part of the greeting Grandma made me memorize.

"What Grandma's saying is that we can offer you a last wish," I said, trying to smooth things over a bit. "If there's something you didn't have a chance to take care of or a message you'd like to send, we're here to try to help you complete it."

"Oh." Alma sniffed. "That's nice enough, I suppose."

"This magical one-of-a-kind opportunity that we offer for free?" Grandma crossed her arms as she stared down at Alma. "I'd say it's pretty nice."

"And you couldn't be bothered to tell me about this during that interminably long funeral planning session you made me sit through?"

Grandma rolled her eyes. "This will be a strange concept for you, but there's such a thing as a *secret*—"

"I know what a secret is," Alma huffed at her. "I'm saying it would have been nice to have some time to think about things instead of having it sprung on me after the fact. It's a lot to take in." She glanced over at me. "So. I'm really dead, then."

"Yes, ma'am," I said softly. I didn't add an "I'm sorry" or anything. I was learning that when we Woke someone, what they most appreciated was simple facts. It made it easier for the truth of their situation to sink in. Then they could wrap their brain around a last wish.

"And you'll help me sort out anything I need finishing?" From what Grandma said, Alma had been ill for a while and had done all of the usual preplanning, but something always fell through the cracks.

"Within reason," Grandma said quickly. "No harming

anyone or sending nasty messages. No vandalism or other crimes."

"Honestly, Bev," Alma said, frowning. "What do you take me for?"

"It's just the usual terms and conditions, ma'am," I reassured her.

Her lips twisted as she nodded to herself. "I need help with my Morris," she said. "I couldn't bear the thought of finding a new home for him while I was still alive. I wanted him with me. My niece will be taking care of closing the house, but she's allergic to cats. I don't want him to be without a family. She'll be in a rush to get back home and I . . ."

"We'll make sure he gets placed somewhere nice," I said.

"And ask the Horticultural Society to name a prize after me for the garden show," Alma added. "To recognize my many achievements over the years."

"The Alma Waters Award for Second Place?" Grandma quipped and I nudged her with my foot, trying to get us back on track. This was *absolutely* not following our usual protocols. "I'll ask," she said. "But no promises."

"And—"

"It's called *a* last wish," Grandma grumbled. "Singular. Hurry it up. There's a time limit here."

"It's for my funeral," Alma said quietly. "One little thing."

I gave her hand an encouraging squeeze. "What would you like?"

A wicked gleam came into her eye. "Digestive biscuits," she said.

"What," Grandma said flatly.

"You heard me. I want digestive biscuits served at the funeral," she said. "Not the kind with chocolate, either. The *plain* ones."

Grandma's face turned red as she curled a perfectly lined lip and I bit back a laugh. Growing up in a funeral home, I'd witnessed plenty of rituals for saying farewell to a loved one. But the Jones family had one golden rule:

A life could *not* be celebrated with substandard cookies.

"Digestive biscuits?" Grandma Bev snarled. I knew from a previous cookie rant that she considered them to be one step away from a coaster. Different ingredients, same result.

"Consider it my parting gift," Alma said, her smile turning a bit damp. "You old bat."

Grandma stopped short, barking out a surprised laugh. She shook her head and groaned. "Fine," she said. "Meddlesome biddy."

"Okay." Alma settled back on the table with a sigh.

"That's all." She closed her eyes. "Give me a minute to picture something else so your face isn't the last thing I see before I go."

"Good*bye*, Alma," Grandma said, poking lightly at her leg.

Alma's lips twitched. "Goodbye, Bev."

Eyes a little moist, Grandma nodded at me, giving me a chance to finish things off without her walking me through it. I concentrated on a gradual transition, picturing the golden light loosening its hold on Alma's spark and flowing back into my hands.

Alma let out a slow breath and her grip relaxed. I set her hand gently down at her side as her spark faded, letting the connection between us dissolve.

"Well done, sweetheart." Grandma touched my shoulder with her usual *pat, pat, pat* and drew me in for a little hug. "You're getting better at this."

"You think so?"

"Without a doubt." She reached out to straighten Alma's clothes and tidy her hair before placing the sheet back over her. "Your father would be proud," she said softly.

She said so every time, but I never got tired of hearing it.

The power hummed in my chest like it always did after

a Waking, taking a bit of time to get settled. "Do we have anyone else coming in today?" I asked. "I could do five more of these."

Grandma pursed her lips, taking her time putting the stools away before answering me. "It might seem like that now," she said eventually. "But there's a limit to what we can do. You can't exhaust yourself." She paced around the room, tidying things that were already in their proper places.

"That's why it's so important to learn control," Grandma said. "It can be tempting to try to do more. To push beyond those limits, but you *can't*. Do you understand?" She was piercing me with an intense look so I nodded even though I didn't. Not really.

What exactly was the limit?

What would happen if I did push beyond it?

The questions running through my brain must have been plain as day since Grandma squinted at me and sighed. "Not today," she said. "Training follows a carefully planned schedule. You'll have your answers in the end. It's a—"

"Process," I said, nodding again. "I know."

That earned me another *pat, pat, pat* on the shoulder, and I knew the subject was closed for now. "What's your plan for Alma's last wish?" I asked her. "Or *wishes*, I guess."

"I'll take care of talking to the Horticultural Society," Grandma said as we headed toward the stairs. "And you can tell your mother she needs to pick up some *digestive biscuits*."

"Can't bring yourself to go pick them up in person?" I laughed as we reached the main floor.

"Stop." A pained look crossed over her face. "Don't laugh at your poor old grandmother." She swatted at me when I couldn't stop.

Finally, when I'd caught my breath, I remembered Alma's most important wish. "What about Morris?"

"I was thinking . . ." Grandma steered me toward the next set of stairs that led to our living area. "That you're ready to handle a last wish delivery on your own."

Wait, what? I stopped in my tracks. She pushed me forward, up to her room, as I tried to process. This was new.

Last fall, Dr. Vernon told Grandma that she needed to slow down. Something about her heart and her blood pressure. She'd waved away all of my questions, saying it was quite manageable and not to worry myself. She only had to make a few changes.

Small ones like resting more often and going for more checkups throughout the year. She stepped aside and let Mom and my stepdad, Alex, fully take over running the funeral home. Grandma still helped out a little bit, but her main focus was on last wishes and training me.

All of the last wish stuff got moved out of the office and up to her bedroom. There was a tiny desk in the corner where her ancient typewriter sat with the fancy, creamy cardstock that she used in a stack beside it. Because "last wishes deserve fancy paper, Kimmy." And all of the family journals sat on a bookshelf in another corner. Records of every Jones and their Wakings going back generations.

Not that I'd been allowed to touch any of it.

Up until now.

"You can type up the letter," Grandma continued. "And deliver it after the funeral."

"By *myself*?" Dealing with alive people was always more daunting for some reason.

"You've watched me do it plenty of times and this will be your responsibility sooner rather than later," she said patiently. "Put down exactly what Alma said about her cat, and when you take the letter to her niece, you can let her know that this was part of Alma's funeral package. That she wished for it to be delivered after her service. Then she'll know what Alma wants and she can handle it."

"But how will I know if she finds Morris a nice home?"

"We do the best that we can with the last wishes, Kimmy," she said, walking over to sit down on her bed.

"But we also can't draw too much attention to ourselves. You have to trust that the note will be enough."

A little voice in my brain wanted to push back because I still didn't understand why we couldn't do *more*. We usually limited people to one wish. Alma was the only exception I'd seen so far. But why didn't we sit with them for as long as it took to get their messages out to everyone they needed to speak with? Why not make *sure* their wishes were honored?

Shouldn't we try anything and everything if it made someone's death a little bit easier?

But I didn't ask because I knew what Grandma would say.

I'd heard it during my training far too many times. "We're just a small part of a larger journey for people. We don't intervene. We don't get too involved. For our safety as much as anything else."

This time my small part would have to be writing up Alma's last wish and hoping it would help her niece find the best home for Morris.

Grandma lay back on her pillows. "Alma tuckered me out," she said. "I'm going to rest my eyes for a bit. Let me know when you're done."

She'd been "resting her eyes" more often lately. And sitting down in viewing rooms while directing my hauling around flower arrangements or setting up seating. Having private talks with Mom and Alex.

I wish I knew *exactly* what Dr. Vernon had told her.

If she was sick like Alma had been.

With so many questions today and zero answers to show for it, there was only one thing I *could* do. I sat down at the tiny desk and started typing.

Chapter Two

Alma's funeral was held a few days later on a sunny Saturday afternoon. Her service was one of the—I didn't want to say happier ones—but it was undeniably a celebration of her long life. People shared funny stories and laughed while they hugged.

And it was well attended, which always pleased Grandma.

Though no one ate the digestive biscuits, which did not please Grandma.

My stepdad, Alex, dumped them into the garbage with a flourish while we were cleaning up, whispering "diGESTive BIScuits!" at me in a perfect, high-pitched imitation.

"Please," my mom hissed as she brushed by us, carrying

a huge bouquet. "Get those out of sight before we have to sit through another rant."

Alex kept me laughing as I swept up and he cleared the snack table, singing a little tune under his breath where the only lyrics were variations on "diGEStive BIScuits!"

Until Grandma heard and grabbed the broom to chase us both out.

I kept a hold of the letter until Friday so I wouldn't be intruding too soon after the funeral. Alma's niece had mentioned she was staying until at least the following Monday to get the house packed up. Heading out after school into the brisk March wind, I walked the few blocks to Alma's place and practiced my speech in my head. This had to go perfectly. I wanted Grandma to know that I was capable of carrying *all* aspects of our family legacy. Of continuing on where she would leave off.

I came up to Alma's cute little white-and-black cottage and knocked. A tired-looking woman with a runny red nose that stood out against her tan skin and brown hair slung up in a messy bun answered the door. "May I help you?"

My mind went blank.

"Hi, hello." I stumbled through the greeting. My first last-wish errand and I was already messing it up. "My name is Kimberly Jones," I said. "I'm with the Jones Family Funeral Home."

"Little young to be working already, aren't you?" she asked with a faint smile.

No such thing in our family. "My grandmother asked me to deliver this." I held out the letter to her. "It was left with the paperwork when your aunt did her preplanning. It's a note with some of her final wishes."

"Oh." She made a surprised noise as she accepted the envelope.

"We're very sorry for your loss," I said.

She called me back as I turned to leave. "Would you like a drink before you go?" she asked. "Kitchen's kind of bare, but I think I spotted some hot chocolate packages on a top shelf."

I didn't want it getting back to Grandma that I was rude to a last-wish recipient so I agreed and followed her inside, sighing in relief at the cozy warmth.

The woman dropped the envelope on a side table and headed toward the kitchen. "I'll put the kettle on."

"Thank yo—ah!" I jumped when something brushed against my leg.

"Mrrreow?" An extremely large, extremely fluffy brown tabby cat was winding its way through my legs, purring up a storm.

"That's Morris," the woman called from the doorway. "I'm surprised to see him out in the open. He's been hiding away ever since—" She cut herself off. I knew what she meant, anyway. Ever since Alma passed. "I'm Ellen, by the way," she said, clearing her throat. "I just realized I never introduced myself."

"It's nice to meet you both," I said.

The kettle boiled and Ellen headed back into the kitchen, returning with two steaming mugs of hot chocolate. I thanked her when she handed one to me.

"Let's see what Aunt Alma has to say," she said, striding to a side table to retrieve the envelope. I really shouldn't be here for this. Grandma was pretty clear about that part. It was supposed to be a private moment, but I had a mouthful of steaming liquid and she was already unfolding the note.

"She wants me to find a home for Morris." Ellen sighed. I tried to look like I wasn't in fact the person who'd typed up the letter and knew exactly what it said. "He can't stay with me," she continued, pointing at her red nose and sniffling.

Morris flopped down and showed me his belly so I leaned down to give him a careful scritch because cat law demanded it.

"I don't even know anyone in this town," Ellen said,

frowning at the two of us. "I'm only here to pack up Alma's house. Once I get it on the market, I'm headed back home. Is there an animal shelter around here?"

That was *not* what Alma had been hoping for with her last wish. I had to steer this in a better direction, for her sake and Morris's. "Do you know any of her friends? Maybe one of them would be willing to take him?"

Ellen watched Morris as he walked in little circles before settling on my feet. "Or," she said, a hopeful look coming into her eyes. "Maybe there's another option?"

I stood in front of my house while Morris meeped from inside the cat carrier in my arms.

The thing was, how could I say no?

How could we go to all the trouble of making Alma's last wish known and then *not* do everything to help it succeed? Letting Morris go to the shelter was the complete opposite of placing him in a loving home. Not that the Basbridge Animal Shelter didn't do everything in their power to try to find homes for all of the animals that came through their doors, but they were still a temporary place. Not a *home*.

My house was a home. It even said so on the sign over the door.

And I could give Morris lots of love.

I thought Alma would probably be pleased by this turn of events. Not in the least because Grandma Bev was going to be enormously displeased by it.

It might have been a snap decision, but I knew in my gut it was the right one. Now I had to convince Mom, Alex, and Grandma. I stepped through the front door and Grandma was there to meet me. "That's a cat," she said, staring at the carrier in my arms. "Why do you have a cat? Julia? She has a cat!"

Mom came down the stairs with Alex on her heels. "Kimmy, honey? What's going on?"

"Alma's niece is allergic and she has to leave soon and she doesn't know anyone in town so she was going to send Morris to a shelter. But Alma said specifically in her last wish that she wanted him to go to a loving home and so I agreed to take him." I took a much-needed breath.

"Kimmy." Grandma side-eyed the carrier. "We can't personally grant every last wish."

"You keep telling me to trust myself—"

"Within the rules," she shot back. "You *know* how we work. Choices like this are a slippery slope. You have to learn where to draw the line."

"Bev," Mom said and Grandma brushed her off.

"We facilitate, but—"

"Bev—"

"We don't *intervene*—"

"She can keep the cat, Bev." Mom interrupted her, bringing Grandma up short. "You decided that she was old enough to deliver a last wish on her own, and this is how she decided to handle it." Mom smiled at me. "You'll be responsible for him, right, sweetie?"

I nodded vigorously at her, careful not to dislodge Morris.

"May I please speak to you in the office?" Grandma asked Mom before walking stiffly out of the foyer.

"Be right back," Mom said, ruffling my hair before following Grandma. "Talk to Alex about what supplies we need to pick up," she tossed over her shoulder at us.

Talking to Alex about litter boxes and types of cat toys wasn't enough of a distraction to cover the conversation-slash-argument that was happening in the office.

"She needs to learn," Grandma was insisting.

"She's also a kid," Mom replied. "Not everything has to be about training and using '*the gift*.' She has a life outside of that."

This was familiar territory.

For as long as I could remember, Grandma and Mom had disagreed over how to manage things. Everything from the funeral home to me. That wasn't anything new.

"Two strong personalities" was Alex's diplomatic way of putting it.

Ever since I'd started my training, though, it was less little disagreements and more actual arguments. Both of them tugging in opposite directions with me in the middle.

Mom always reminding me that there was more to my life than my power and making sure I was keeping up with school and hanging out with my friends.

Grandma always stealing me away to practice. As prickly as she could be sometimes, I loved training with her. It was *our* time. I was the only one left to learn about the family power, and she always made space for me to learn about my dad, too.

It was a way for me to stay connected to him.

I knew there was more to my life than our power, but I liked how it made us special. Like we were part of something bigger. I didn't know how to explain that to Mom without fueling the friction between them.

"And she's *my* kid," Mom continued. "It's not your place to say whether or not she can have a pet."

"It's not about having a pet. It's about *boundaries*," Grandma shot back. "She has to respect them."

"Of course she's pushing boundaries," Mom said. "She's Nathan's child. We knew this would happen and I think it's time—"

"There's a process. You know I'm being careful and watching her every move—"

"But she still needs to know exactly what she's getting into," Mom interrupted her. "And I thought you would tell her by now."

Hang on. What did *that* mean?

"Kimmy will know everything she needs to know," Grandma said. "At the right time—"

"I don't *care* about the process!" Mom exclaimed. "Nathan's gone and *I* can't train her. I don't have all the answers. They have to come from you and I'm worried you're leaving it too late."

"I'm well aware of that, Julia," Grandma said, voice tight.

"Hey." Alex took the cat carrier from my arms, startling me out of my eavesdropping. "Let's go upstairs and look up cat trees and see what we can convince your mom to go for. Maybe one of those floor-to-ceiling ones?"

I reluctantly followed him up, missing the rest of what sounded like more than just a conversation between two strong personalities.

What weren't they telling me?

✳ ✳ ✳

Dinner was a tense affair, with Alex trying to keep a conversation going between Mom and Grandma, both equally terse, while I focused on studying them for more clues.

Neither of them gave me much to go on.

I had to give Alex credit for the attempt at normalcy. He'd moved in with us a few years ago when he and Mom got married and was shockingly good at rolling with our family's . . . eccentricities, but even he couldn't work miracles.

Grandma had a very expressive silent eyebrow conversation with Mom as we packed up the leftovers. It ended with Mom nodding her head emphatically in my direction. Very subtle.

Alex kept himself busy with the dishes and I didn't dare make eye contact with him in case we both started giggling.

"Mr. Railings came in this afternoon, Kimmy," Grandma said, clearing her throat. "Would you like to go downstairs for some more training?"

"Yes, please," I said immediately. It'd be easier to corner her for answers down in the prep room.

"Let me know when you're done," Mom said. "Alex and I will start working on him."

I followed Grandma to the prep room, where she took

her time getting set up, being extra particular about where everything went.

More lights on that side, Kimmy.

Move the stool this way.

No, actually, put it back.

Finally, she deemed everything ready to go with Mr. Railings laid out between us. After following the usual steps to connect with my power, I took his hand and searched for the warmth, but it was like reaching into a cold, empty space.

No spark.

I reached a little further with the power. To double-check. I never wanted to miss anyone and if I stretched—

"Kimmy." Grandma's voice sliced through, startling me out of my efforts. "You've checked enough. Is there a spark?"

Shaking my head at Grandma, I set Mr. Railings's hand back at his side.

"No unfinished business then, Ken?" She tilted her head as she looked down at him. "I can never decide if that means someone's very lucky or very boring."

"Grandma!"

She shrugged as she covered him back up. "It's a tidy life that has no loose ends."

She wasn't wrong. I couldn't imagine not having one last thing you wanted to say or do and I couldn't decide if such a clean slate was sad or not.

"Quite the rarity," Grandma said, turning to put away the lights. Her tone was pleasant, but her face was still tight.

Maybe it was thinking about unfinished business or the fact that I was between Grandma and the stairs, but now seemed like as good a time as any to get those answers.

Unless she tried to make a break for the elevator.

"What were you and Mom fighting about earlier?" I blurted out.

"We weren't fighting—"

"I *heard* you." I planted myself on one of the stools and stared her down. "All that stuff about Dad and boundaries and telling me something? What was that about?"

She ran a hand through her silvery bob and sighed. "No one wants to let me follow the process." Grandma grabbed the other stool and rolled it over to sit beside me. "I have everything mapped out, you know," she said. "To share our history with you and expand your training as appropriate. Rushing these things can do more harm than good."

"I think I've done pretty well handling everything so far," I said with a little shrug. "Is whatever you have to tell me really so bad?"

"Yes," Grandma said bluntly. "Because it's about how our power killed your father."

Chapter Three

I sat frozen on my stool, unable to form words.

Of all the things I thought she'd say, "our power killed your father" hadn't even made the list. "Why—why was that a secret? When were you going to tell me? How—"

Grandma held up a hand to cut off my torrent of questions. "I wanted to you to be focused solely on learning and building a solid foundation of control," she said. "I didn't want to distract you—"

"With all of the deadly details?" I scoffed, flinging my arms out.

"Do not raise your voice at me." Grandma pointed a stern finger in my face.

Raising my voice was arguably an acceptable response

to the situation, but it wouldn't get me anywhere with Grandma. I slumped back on my stool. "I'm sorry," I muttered. "Will you tell me now?"

"No more interruptions. Please," she said. "I don't want to have to repeat this story."

I pressed my lips together tight.

"When the power first manifested in our family," Grandma began, her back ramrod straight as she stared off into the distance, "it was strong and wild. Dangerous to use. The cost was . . . high."

"What—"

Grandma shook her head at me. Right. No interruptions.

"Luckily, our ancestors found a solution," Grandma said. "They asked another magical family to use their powers to cap ours."

"What do you mean 'cap'?" The question slipped out before I could stop it, but Grandma allowed it.

"Limitations," she said. "It's why we have to be touching someone to form the connection and why we can only hold that connection for a few minutes."

My brain tripped over the implications of that. Had the past Jones family members walked around Waking people long distance or something?

"Our family moved to Basbridge shortly after that,"

Grandma continued, unaware or possibly just ignoring the fact that she was blowing my mind. "It was a way to stay under the radar. There were no other magic users here, and the house has extra protections on it to help hide us."

"Why does that matter?" I asked her, trying to catch up and process all of this new information. "Wouldn't knowing other people with magic be helpful?"

"Not for us," Grandma said, shaking her head. "A power like ours is rare. Tempting. Something many would want to exploit or even kill for."

"Is that what happened to Dad?" I almost didn't want to hear the answer at this point. "Did someone kill him for the power?"

"No one killed him," Grandma assured me. She rolled her stool back a bit to lean against the storage cupboard with a sigh. She closed her eyes for a moment before looking over at me. "I *did* train him. Made sure he knew about the limitations, the risks, and I thought that was enough. I gave him space to embrace his gift and I didn't know what he was doing until it was too late."

"What was he doing?" I whispered.

"Testing the limits," she said. "He wanted to understand the full spectrum of our capabilities. Your father thought there could be other aspects to our power—other ways to help people that we weren't aware of. He increased his efforts after your grandfather died and kept it up even after your arrival."

My stomach did a slow turn at the thought of asking, but we'd already come this far.

And I needed to know.

"How did that end up killing him?"

"He pushed so hard one day that he had a stroke, and he died," Grandma said. "He was twenty-six years old." Grandma's voice broke over those words and her eyes filled with tears.

I leapt up to give her a hug. There was nothing I could say to make it better, but I held on as tight as I could.

"I brought him back," she mumbled into my hair. I shuffled around to lean into her side and she kept an arm around me. "So you and Julia and I could say goodbye. I know you don't remember; you were only a year and a half. But your mother and I—it was good to be able to talk to him."

"Did he have a last wish?" For all the stories I'd heard about him, that was another detail Grandma had never shared.

"Ah." Grandma detached me from her side and headed over to the computer on the desk at the far side of the room.

"He did," she said. "He asked to record a video for you."

I scrambled after her. "There's a video?"

She clicked around until she found the file and opened it. A rectangle popped up and all of a sudden—

There was my dad.

He sat in what was clearly the prep room. The video was a bit wobbly as he held the phone, and I could see the edge of Grandma's shoulder every once in a while beside him.

"Hi, Kimmy, sweetheart," he said. "I'm sorry—I'm *so* sorry that I'm not going to be there with you. I love you so much. I know you're going to do amazing things."

He took a shaky breath.

"More amazing things than your old dad," he said. "Remember to always listen to your grandma, okay? Promise me that." He stared intensely into the camera. "This family power . . . it can be overwhelming. She'll help you through it. I know she can be cranky, but trust her. Be good and *listen*."

Grandma grumbled something in the background of the video and he laughed quietly.

"Give your mom hugs for me. Every day. And know that she's giving you hugs from me, too. And I better not see any of you for a long, long time. Okay. That's all. I love you."

The screen froze on his face as the video ended.

That was my dad.

Talking right to me.

I didn't have any real memories of him. There were videos and pictures of him with me as a baby and with Mom, but nothing face-to-face like that.

I already knew from those pictures that I didn't look like him. Not really. I had his eyes, blue and wide, but for the most part I looked like Mom. Both of us short and round with pale skin, red cheeks, and redder hair. Dad took after Grandma; tall and lanky with dark brown hair although Grandma's was fully gray now.

Mom always said I had his smile too, but she never told me I had his laugh.

What else would I never know?

Part of me wished Grandma *hadn't* shown me that video. I missed my dad every day, but in the way you missed someone you'd never got to meet. After watching that, he was more real than ever before.

Now I missed him in a whole new way.

Stepping away from the computer, I swiped at my eyes. "That's it?" I asked Grandma. "That's the whole thing?" Minutes when I should have had years.

"It was all we had time for," she said with an apologetic

smile. "He spent most of his last-wish time making sure he left a message for you."

"I'd rather have him," I burst out. "Is this what it's like for everybody else? When we pass along the last wishes?" I never thought we'd be hurting people.

Grandma frowned at me, settling back on her stool. "What do you mean?"

"What's the point? What are we really giving anyone?" I pointed at the computer. That message wasn't enough. "Videos and letters aren't replacing their loved ones. I thought—I thought we were helping, but they don't make it better. They don't fix anything."

I thought when we passed on last wishes, we were filling people up with the warmth of their loved ones. Giving them closure. Something to hold on to, at least.

This—it wasn't *enough*.

"It's not about replacement," she said, gesturing for me to take a seat. I stood my ground, holding my arms tight across my middle as a buzzing energy filled my veins. The lights, the smell of the prep room, Grandma's stare; everything was too much. I gripped the sides of my shirt and tried to anchor myself in place. To breathe.

"This is what I've been trying to show you," Grandma said quietly. "There's no fixing death. You know that, growing up here. And I *know* you know that's not what last wishes are truly for."

"They're to offer a small piece of comfort," I recited with a groan as I scrubbed a hand down my face. "But what if we're only reminding them of what's been lost?"

Grandma sat for a moment before nodding. "Sometimes it takes a while before a reminder becomes a comfort," she said. "I remember one last wish I delivered was from a mother to her daughter. She wanted her to know that there were bulbs tucked away in the garage because she was worried that they'd be overlooked. Three years I drove by and no dahlias."

"Did she forget?"

"No, she needed time," Grandma said. "That fourth year, I drove by and there they were, blooming in her daughter's garden. She planted them when she was ready for the reminder." She came over to me and wrapped an arm around my shoulder. "The last wish didn't fix anything, but it did help eventually."

Grandma gave me a squish, an unspoken *do you get it now?* and I shrugged.

"I don't know about you," she said "but I could go for some cookies. Get the lights, would you, sweetie?" She did her little *pat, pat, pat* on my arm and headed for the stairs.

Like it was a normal night and she hadn't upended most of what I thought I knew about our family.

Conversation over, I guess.

For now.

Chapter Four

I took my time making sure the prep room was neat and tidy before I left.

The funeral home itself was more than a hundred and fifty years old, but the prep room had been remodeled a few times so it was sleek and up-to-date. I wiped down every surface until it shined, hoping I'd be less unsettled by the time I was done.

Soon the place was sparkling.

I looked around.

It could use a sweep, too.

The door at the top of the stairs opened. "Kimmy?" Mom called down. "Are you coming?"

"Yep, one sec." Shutting off the lights, I took a deep

breath and headed upstairs to the kitchen. Mom and Grandma were sitting at the table, watching me as I made my way into the room. There were three glasses of milk and a plate of Grandma's special cookies in front of them. A peace offering.

I decided to allow it. At least everyone's mouths would be too full of baked goods to share any more earth-shattering news.

Joining them at the table, I snagged a cookie and bit into it with a sigh. Nothing beat the chocolate-butterscotch-and-just-the-right-amount-of-crispy goodness of Grandma's special cookies. She had yet to share the full recipe with me, but she kept the kitchen well stocked.

Having a bad day? Come home and grab a special cookie.

Having a great day? Cookie.

Before she stepped back, it wasn't unusual to walk into the kitchen and find Grandma in there helping someone make their final arrangements over a cup of tea and a plate of cookies.

I could never put my finger on why they tasted so good. Another family secret.

"This is the last of them and we're out of flour," Grandma said. "I'll go to the store in the morning to pick some up so let me know if you need anything else, Julia."

We finished our snack quietly, everyone lost in their own thoughts, before Mom started making noise about it being time for me to get ready for bed.

I headed upstairs with everything I'd learned today still leaving me off balance. Grandma puffed her way up behind me, snagging my elbow and steering me toward her room.

"One last thing," she said as I tried to pull away.

"Can it wait?" I asked. Today had already been a *lot*.

"It'll be worth it," she promised. "Trust me."

Turned out, even huge revelations couldn't shake my trust in Grandma because I immediately followed her through her doorway. It paid off when she made a beeline for the bookshelf. *The* bookshelf. The one with the Jones family journals on it. The ones I was allowed to look at from two feet away and never, ever touch.

Grandma plucked four books off of the top shelf and came back to stand in front of me.

"Now that you're further into your training," she said. "It's time to start your own journal." She handed me the first book—a leather-bound journal with a *J* cut into the front. "And I think you're ready to begin reading our history." She handed me the other books.

Their covers were nearly identical to the first one, but

the edges of the pages inside were worn and speckled with ink. I flipped one open and let out a little gasp at the name on the first page. *Nathan Jones*. Dad's journals.

"It'll take you some time to read through them all," she said with a nod to the *large* collection of diaries on the shelves. "But I think these might be the best place to start."

"Wow." I traced a finger over my father's handwriting. One more connection. "Thank you, Grandma."

"Mind you take good care of them," she said, looking more pleased than stern as I nodded vigorously.

Later, once I was tucked up in bed with Morris and *my* journal, working away on the first entry, there was a knock on the door. Mom came in cautiously, shutting it behind her.

"Hey," she said as sat down on the end of the bed. "I know that must have been a shock. How are you doing with everything?"

"You really want me to answer that?"

"Yes!" She grabbed my ankle through the covers and gave it a shake. "Talk to me, please."

"The video of Dad was . . ."

"Tough?"

"Yeah." Understatement. "I don't understand why no one told me any of this before now," I said, and she nodded with an understanding hum. "Grandma explained her reasons, but what about *you*?"

"At first, you were too little," Mom said. "I didn't know how to explain what had happened to him in a way you'd understand."

I could see that. "But what about later?"

"As you got older, your grandma and I fought about it quite a few times, but eventually I realized she was right," Mom continued. "It was important for you to have an understanding of the power and a certain level of control first. We agreed to wait until you started training. To follow the process."

"You fought about it?"

"Big time," Mom said, eyes going wide. "I was torn. I wanted you to love exploring your power as much as your dad did. It's a gift. Your gift. But at the same time, I was scared you could end up following his path."

I hadn't thought about what it had been like from Mom's perspective. "I'm surprised you even let me train."

"Oh, I thought about taking you and leaving," she said.

"Seriously?" I couldn't imagine not growing up in the funeral home with Grandma. "What made you decide to stay?"

Mom tucked her feet up on the bed and curled in

beside Morris. "I didn't want us to leave your grandma all alone," Mom said. "And even if we had left, the magic is a literal part of you. I didn't want to risk you growing up and figuring out how to tap into it without training. That would've been more dangerous. Plus, there's the protection the house offers."

"Grandma said something about that," I said. A shield? "What does it mean?"

"I'm trying to remember what your dad told me," she said. "Something about runes being carved into the wood as the house was built. The only magic users who can enter the house are members of the Jones family or the family that helped set up the protections."

That sounded fascinating, and on any other day, I'd want to learn more. I sighed. Everything she'd said made sense. I could understand, at least a little bit, but—

"I still don't like that you both kept something so huge from me." I fiddled with the blanket as I tried to sift through my thoughts. "It made me miss Dad a lot," I said. "And I'm kind of upset with *him*, too. It's weird—" I cut myself off, not sure how to continue that thought.

"What's weird?" Mom prompted gently.

"There's this whole other side of our power that I've

never known about." What had been so cool and special was now something dangerous. Was it allowed to be both?

She covered my hand with hers when I started picking at a thread. "Do you want to stop?" she asked me. "Or take a break maybe?"

"I don't know," I confessed. Mom had always said it was an option, but I'd never considered it before.

She let that sit between us while she petted Morris and his rumbling purrs filled the room. I worked up the nerve to ask the question that had been eating at me for the past hour.

"Were *you* mad at Dad?" Mom looked up with a frown. "When he died," I clarified.

She froze, caught off guard, but if today was a day for answers then I might as well tick all of the boxes.

"I was," she said slowly. "For a long time. But that wasn't the part I wanted to hold on to when I remembered him. And I never wanted to pass that anger on to you so I worked through it. Having you and your grandma around helped a lot." She nudged at my legs. "It's okay if you're upset too right now. I'll help you work through it. Whatever you need."

I had no clue what I needed.

"Grandma gave me my journal," I said, ready to be

done with this topic for now. Thankfully, Mom rolled with the subject change.

"Oooh, adding to the family history," she said. "That's an exciting milestone."

"And she said I could start reading the others."

Mom's eyes went wide. "That's huge," she said. "I've yet to be granted that honor."

Grandma was pretty firm on it being a "Joneses by blood only" privilege.

"She gave me Dad's to start with," I said, holding the journals out to Mom. She took one carefully and stroked a gentle finger down the spine.

"I remember him writing in these," she said with a fond smile before handing it back. "It'll be a great way for you get to know your dad more. I'm excited for you."

Morris stood up all of sudden and meeped at us. He headbutted Mom's shoulder before turning in a circle and lying back down again. We both burst into giggles.

"I am sorry, you know, for the random pet adoption," I said. "I didn't mean to cause trouble."

"Oh, honey, no," she said. "In the future, please talk to us first before diving into a big decision like that, but I understand why you did it."

Glad *she* did. "Grandma's not marking it down as a successful first last-wish run."

"You were trying to do a good thing," Mom said firmly. "I hope that's what you always try to do. Whenever possible."

"I'll remind you of that when I end up bringing home more strays," I said.

"'When,' she says." Mom laughed as she tweaked my nose. "Don't stay up too late reading. Lights-out in ten, okay?"

"Okay," I agreed. "Night, Mom. Love you."

She leaned over and pulled me into a hug, squeezing extra tight. "Love you, too," she said. "So much." After one final cuddle, she left, shutting the door behind her, and I cracked open the first of Dad's journals.

Touching a finger to the first page, I traced the little indents made with each letter. Morris crawled his way up to tuck into my side. "Listen to this," I whispered to him.

Hi. I'm Nathan Jones.

I'm twelve years old and I'm kind of freaking out. My mom is teaching me how to bring people back from the dead. It's cool, but also very VERY strange.

I couldn't help chuckling.

You're not wrong, Dad. You're definitely not wrong.

Turning the pages, I tsked when I found a few spots where pages had been ripped out. That was not treating your journal with respect, Nathan Jones. Hope Grandma never caught him doing that.

I kept reading and had just started to nod off when my door creaked open again.

"Lights out, Kimmy," Grandma Bev whispered as she poked her head into my room. She fussed at the sight of me with the journal on my bed and hurried over to gather it up. "I expected you to take care of this, not sleep on it."

"I was going to put it on the shelf—"

"With your eyes closed? Impressive." Grandma set the journal on my side table and sat down on the bed beside me. She reached out to brush the hair off my face, her gaze softening. "Good read so far?"

"Dad's talking about how strange bringing people back from the dead is." I smiled.

"I've been doing this for fifty-eight years and I still think that too sometimes," she said with a laugh, patting my leg before standing up with a groan.

Fifty-eight years. That was a lot of Wakings and last wishes.

And goodbyes.

"Hey, Grandma?"

"Hmm?" She paused in the doorway.

"Thanks for sharing Dad's journal with me," I said. "And for teaching me."

"Nothing else I'd rather do. You've been an excellent student."

My face must have betrayed my doubts about that because she laughed softly and leaned against the frame. "You've been putting in a lot of training time this week," Grandma said. "Why don't we take a break tomorrow and do something wild."

"Like what?" I couldn't wait to hear Grandma's idea of something wild.

"Like go see a movie and sneak in all our own snacks. I'll have fresh cookies in the morning. We can take those." Her face creased into a satisfied grin like it was the most evil genius plan ever.

I had no arguments. It was a great plan.

"I'm in," I said.

"Okay, then. The sooner you get to sleep, the sooner we adventure." She blew me a kiss. "Goodnight, sweetheart."

"Night."

I rolled over and turned off my lamp as she shut the

door. Today had been unexpectedly overwhelming, but tomorrow was a new day. One full of adventure, according to Grandma.

The thought put a smile on my face as I drifted off to sleep.

Chapter Five

I woke up with the energy of *two* Kimmys.

Learning deep dark family secrets really made you sleep like a rock.

I wasn't going to question it. Today was special cookies and a movie adventure with Grandma. We'd earned some fun. We could start working through the rest of it tomorrow.

Throwing on some clothes, I grabbed my phone, blinking when I saw the time. Hard to believe I'd managed to sleep until ten am without Mom or Grandma hauling me out of bed.

Stepping into the hallway, I paused. Something was off.

The house was too quiet.

It was Saturday morning. Usually, Alex was clattering

around in the kitchen, singing horribly out of tune. Grandma should be back from her Saturday morning shopping and on to vacuuming the whole first level.

But the only thing I could hear was Morris snoring from the foot of the bed.

Did *everyone* sleep in?

I tiptoed farther down the hall and stopped at the top of the stairs to listen. No snores floating out from any of the other bedrooms. Not a peep from the bathroom.

Leaning forward, I caught the edge of a low conversation drifting up from the kitchen. At least there were *some* signs of life. I headed down the stairs to find out what was going on and tried to ignore the growing dread that I wouldn't like the answer.

Mom and Alex sat huddled together at the kitchen table. Mom looked up when I stepped on that one piece of floor by the doorway that always squeaked.

"Kimmy," she said, wiping at her eyes. Drying away *tears*. "You're up early."

"Not really. What's going on?"

Alex pulled out a chair. "Come and have a seat."

I didn't want to have a seat. Walking over there and taking a seat took me one step closer to whatever was happening that made Mom cry.

"Please, honey." She beckoned me over.

I took the seat.

Mom took a deep breath and reached out to hold my hand. "There's no easy way to tell you this," she said. "Your grandma passed away this morning."

"What?" No. That didn't make any sense. "No, she was going to the store this morning. She's making cookies and we're going to the movies later. She's *fine*. Did you try calling her?"

"She did go to the store," Mom said slowly. "But she was found sitting in her car. She had a heart attack, sweetie."

This was all wrong. There was no way—

"She was taking care of herself," I said. "She was resting and taking her medication like she was supposed to."

"With her condition, it was always possible something like this could happen." Mom clutched my hand in hers and I pulled it back.

"One of us should have gone with her. She shouldn't have been alone. Maybe we could have called for help or—"

"Dr. Vernon said it would have happened very quickly," Alex gently cut me off. "There was nothing anyone could have done."

Mom scooched her chair closer to mine so she could

wrap an arm around my shoulders. "Kimmy, this is a lot to take in, and you can ask any questions you need to, okay? I might not have answers, but I'll try."

Piles of questions were swirling around in my brain, but the one that popped out was, "Where is she?"

"Where—oh." Mom sat back in her chair. "She's at the hospital, in the—they have to declare her there and do paperwork. It's procedure."

Of course.

At the hospital.

In the morgue.

Because they have to declare her dead and fill out a death certificate.

I knew that.

Then she'll come back home.

For her funeral.

"Kimmy?" Mom's voice was soft and sounded so very far away.

"I'd like to go back to my room for now," I said, pulling away from her and sliding out of my seat.

"Okay," Mom said. "That's okay. Just—let me know if you need anything."

I nodded and headed for the stairs. Alex's and Mom's quiet voices picked up again as I went to my room. Morris was still lying sprawled across my bed and the sheets were exactly how I'd left them, but nothing—nothing was the same.

And it never would be again.

Mom came up a few hours later and tried to convince me to eat something, but I couldn't. Didn't want to talk, either. She left me a glass of water and went back downstairs.

I knew she would only leave me alone for so long, though.

We were going to have to talk about it.

Not just the Grandma being gone part.

But the part where I'd bring her back.

She managed to hold off until the next day.

When Grandma returned.

Mom coaxed me downstairs where she had a simple lunch of grilled cheese and tomato soup ready. I pushed the spoon around in my bowl and picked at the bread.

"So," Mom began and I braced myself. "We're going to have to . . . prepare Grandma at some point and I need to ask." She took a deep breath. "Do you want to Wake her?"

I didn't even know how to respond to that. *Want* to? Like it was a choice?

"Kimmy, you don't—" Mom scanned my face and sighed. "You need to know that you don't have to. It's *different* when it's a family member. Someone you love. No one is expecting you to do this."

Grandma would.

If she could Wake Dad, I could Wake her.

I was a Jones.

This was what we did.

"It's okay, Mom," I said. "I can do it."

Grandma deserved a last wish and we—we would get a chance to say goodbye.

Once I gave up pretending to eat lunch, we headed down to the prep room together. Mom and Alex stepped back while I set up all the lights exactly how Grandma liked them. I took a deep breath and nodded at Mom.

She pulled the sheet back and there was Grandma.

She looked like herself and *nothing* like herself all at the same time. I tried not to look too closely because it wasn't an image I wanted left in my memories.

Focusing on the job I was there for, I took Grandma's hand and started my breathing exercises. Before I'd even let the first breath out, instead of the usual vibration, there was a sharp *tug, tug, tug* in my chest. My power, ready to go, and stronger than *ever*.

I couldn't help the gasp that slipped out and Mom was instantly by my side.

"Kimmy? Are you okay?"

"Yeah." I waved her off. "The power is acting a little differently, but it's fine." At least I hoped it was. Mom stepped back but still kept close.

Closing my eyes, I pictured that golden ball of light and in a flash, the power spread from my chest, down my arms, and into Grandma. I hadn't even directed it. It rushed out of me.

Tug, tug, tug.

The power pulsed as it swept through Grandma, searching for her spark.

I waited for that familiar spot of warmth to show up.

Any second.

"Kimmy?" Mom whispered.

"Hang on," I muttered.

Maybe it was me. I didn't have Grandma to guide me so I didn't have as much control. Maybe that was why the power was so intense. I needed to focus.

She was there somewhere. She had to be. If I kept looking, if I pushed a little further, I could reach her. I could find her.

I could—

"Kimmy!" Mom's sharp voice cut through my thoughts. "You have to stop."

"I haven't found her spark," I said, gripping Grandma's hand tighter.

"No, you're stopping," Mom said as she pried me away. "Now."

There was one more *tug, tug, tug* in my chest before the power whooshed back, leaving an emptiness in its wake. "Why did you do that?" I cried.

Mom wordlessly grabbed a tissue from the box on the counter and pressed it to my nose. "You were pushing too far," she said, holding it up to show me the spots of blood decorating it.

"I was trying to reach her spark," I snapped. "I was doing something wrong, though, because I couldn't find it. I need to try again."

Mom and Alex exchanged a look. He gave her a little nod before touching my shoulder, kissing the top of my head, and heading upstairs.

"Where's Alex going?" I asked Mom. "Doesn't he want to say goodbye?"

"He'll say his goodbyes later," she said. "But we need to talk. You can't reach Bev's spark, sweetie, and we both know what that means."

"I don't understand." I shook my head fiercely. "There's only no spark if the person doesn't have any unfinished business. Grandma would want to talk to us."

"Kimmy, you looked. If you didn't find her, she's not there."

I stared down at Grandma, quiet and still on the table. "It's *not right*."

"Your grandma is at peace." Mom wrapped an arm around my shoulders, holding me close. "Let's try to make our own peace with that."

What peace was there in something that didn't make any sense at all?

"Do you want to take a minute to talk to her?" Mom asked, reaching out to resettle Grandma's hand and brush some of her hair into place. "Say your own goodbyes?"

"Why should I?" I turned toward the stairs. "Grandma didn't."

I ignored Mom's sigh as I stomped my way back up.

How could Grandma do that?

How could she let her spark move on and pretend she had no unfinished business?

She had *me*.

Chapter Six

Five months after Grandma's funeral and I was still waiting for that moment where things would be normal again, but—

Our family had lost a whole person.

There was nothing normal about that.

I could still *feel* her everywhere. I kept expecting her to come through the door to fill me in on all the gossip from her bridge club.

I never expected to miss *bridge club* gossip.

I hated how the space that she'd held was slowly being filled in ways that didn't fit. Nothing about our home was quite right anymore. In big ways and in small.

Staring down at the cookie table Mom was setting up, I

tried not to sneer at the perfectly nice platter of chocolate chip cookies. Except it was *only* chocolate chip cookies. Grandma Bev would have picked out a complementary assortment. A little something for everyone, she'd say, because details like that were what people remembered about a place.

She'd have slipped a few of her special cookies in, too, but that wasn't something Mom or I could do. Grandma never wrote down the recipe and I still hadn't cracked it.

Mom caught my look and winced apologetically. "I know you don't like it—"

"Having only two kinds last week was bad enough," I grumbled. "People will think we don't *care*."

She stared at me for a moment before shaking her head and muttering something about channeling spirits to criticize her from beyond the grave. "I'll do my best to pick out a whole selection next time I'm at the store, okay? I promise."

I should probably go with her just in case.

Mom looked at her watch and tsked. "I have to get on a call with the Group. Do you mind helping to finish setting up?"

Another space being filled in. Grandma and Grandpa had put the Group together back in the early 2000s. I forgot what the proper name was because everyone always referred to them as the Group. It was an alliance between the Jones Family Funeral Home and a bunch of the surrounding independent funeral homes in Linleydale, Grantleyville, Stoverton, and other nearby towns.

Something to do with sharing resources and pooling their purchasing power to help each other stay afloat against the rise of big funeral corporations? Obviously, it worked since they were still going strong more than twenty years later.

Mom had been joining her at those meetings over the last couple of years. It made the transition a lot smoother when Grandma took her step back from the business last fall. That stung sometimes. Knowing that Mom was able to be fully trained by Grandma in *her* job, but that I still had so much to learn.

And I'd never be taught by her again.

"That's great," Mom said before I could even nod. "Alex is still working on Mr. Melnick downstairs, but Tamsin just arrived so you can join her. Love you! See you soon."

She popped a kiss on top of my head and whizzed away to the office.

Plodding my way over to the main room, I walked in to find Tamsin Bly, the newest employee of the Jones Family

Funeral Home, making a mess of the bouquets.

"That's not how they're supposed to go," I called out.

"Good morning, Tamsin. How are you today?" she singsonged, pausing her work and turning to me with an exaggerated smile on her face. "I'm *wonderful*, Kimmy. Thank you so much for asking!"

"Good morning, Tamsin." I rolled my eyes. "You're setting up the bouquets wrong."

"Okay, yes, I remember you said your grandma liked it done a certain way, but I thought we could try this." She took a step back to study her work. "Something a little more dynamic?"

"She liked it 'a certain way' because putting the taller ones behind makes it easier to see all of the cards," I said, moving in to start rearranging.

"Oh," Tamsin said after a moment. She shrugged. "I guess that makes sense."

I gave myself a little mental *pat, pat, pat* on the back for keeping my growl of frustration on the inside and reminded myself that Tamsin was still fairly new here.

She didn't know the ins and outs like I did.

Mom and Alex hired her a few months ago to have someone who could help out during the week while I was at school. We hadn't crossed paths too often. I'd have to ask Mom to schedule her for more weekends so I could show her the ropes.

I didn't know what her qualifications were, but I had a sneaking suspicion she'd never worked in a funeral home before. I should make sure Mom let me sit in the next time they interviewed someone.

We worked in silence for a few minutes as we put everything in proper order.

"Better?" she asked once we done, holding her arms out in a little "ta-da" pose.

"Almost." I started plucking the lilies out of the various bouquets.

Tamsin snorted. "Okay. Please fill me in on the trade secret behind this?"

"Grandma hates the way they smell," I answered automatically before freezing and looking down at the cluster of flowers clutched in my hand. My job had always been gathering them up and sticking them in a vase by the front door so she could steer clear. I'd kept doing it every week, but now that I was explaining it, I realized no one else cared about the smell.

"I happen to have an extra vase right here," Tamsin said, reaching down to grab one that had been set on the seat of a chair. "Plunk 'em on in."

Grabbing the last couple of lilies, I took the vase and set the whole bundle inside. "I'm gonna—" I jerked a thumb over my shoulder. "Water."

"No problem." Tamsin nodded at the cart of chairs on the other side of the room. "I'll get started on those."

Escaping to the kitchen, I filled the vase with water and set it on the counter.

Should I even bother putting them by the front door?

This was dumb.

I should put them back in the bouquets.

Right?

No.

Smell aside, Grandma always commented on how they brightened up the entryway. That's where they should be. Decision made, I grabbed the vase and marched it out to the small table by the front door.

The light there hit the petals just right and they *did* brighten things up.

"Kimmy?" Mom poked her head out of the office. "Nice flowers. When you're finished with the chairs, will you please ask Tamsin to come see me? We need to go over the schedule for the week. Thank you!"

"Okay," I said to the door that was already closed again. "I'm on it."

No rest at the funeral home.

Maybe *some* things were getting back to normal.

"Mom wants to see you when we're done," I announced when I walked back into the viewing room. Tamsin nodded at me as she kept setting up chairs and I joined her.

We made quick work of it, but both of us were sweating by the end. The air-conditioning could only do so much against the August heat, especially when it was trying to cool down a big, drafty old house.

"Phew!" Tamsin rolled up the sleeves of her dress shirt and fanned her face. I caught a glimpse of a few intricately patterned tattoos inked into her light brown skin.

"Want to see?" She held her arms out, noticing me trying to sneakily take a closer peek.

I nodded and leaned in, trying to make sense of the patterns. "What do they mean?"

Tamsin didn't answer right away and when I looked up, she seemed a bit startled by the question. "Uh, nothing special really. Designs that I thought were cool, that sort of thing."

"Hunh." I went to take another look and—

Wait a minute.

Had one of them gotten brighter? I blinked. Clearly, I was overheated.

"I should get a move on," Tamsin said, rolling her sleeves back down. "Got lots to do today and have to get it done before I turn into a puddle!" She flashed a smile at me as she pulled an elastic off her wrist and piled her sandy brown curls into a bun. "See you later, Kimmy!"

She left me to have her planning meeting with Mom, and I headed back to the kitchen. I had important business of my own to attend to. First on the list was drinking some water.

No more hallucinating for me.

Once that was checked off, I gathered my supplies and laid everything out on the table. Bowls, measuring cups, ingredients, and recipe notes. I'd been keeping track of every attempt.

Maybe number twenty was the time I'd get it right.

Grandma's special cookies were similar to chocolate chip cookies, but they had extras like butterscotch chips and dark chocolate chunks. I knew basically everything she'd used, but I must have the measurements off because each tray I made never tasted *quite right*.

One hour later, I slumped down in my seat and crossed off variation number twenty.

"I thought I heard someone puttering around up here," Alex said as he came through the basement door.

"Do you think I should bother going for attempt number twenty-one?" I sighed.

"What's wrong with twenty?"

I pushed the plate of cookies across the table and he snagged one to take a bite out of. "You know, I think you're getting closer," he said, chewing thoughtfully.

That earned him a flat look. "You say that every time."

"Because every time you're getting closer!" He waved the cookie in the air and patted his tummy. "And every time I get cookies so I definitely vote for try, try again."

"Fine, then we need more eggs," I said, and he grinned.

"Already on the list."

Alex finished off his cookie as I cleaned up the last of my mess. "Ms. Rosini arrived," he said casually. "Do you want to try today? It's your choice. I can adjust when I leave for the crematorium either way."

I knew I should say yes. Waking people was always best done after they'd been cleaned up, but before the embalming process, if that was the route they were taking. Grandma explained it as the window of time when they could Wake and still feel mostly like themselves.

The same rule applied for those going to the crematorium. The window of time wasn't that long, either. I shouldn't leave Ms. Rosini waiting if I didn't want to

Wake her when she was less than her best.

And yet, I hesitated. What was the point? There'd been no sparks in anyone I'd tried to Wake since Grandma. Not a *single one* in months.

The only thing I could ever find was echoes of that old thread with Grandma. A remnant whispering along the edge of my senses. I tried to ignore it, but every attempt at a Waking made me miss her more.

It wasn't helping me figure out the missing sparks conundrum one bit. I'd been contemplating the situation from every angle and as far as I could tell, there were two options.

Option one was that every single person I'd checked actually had no unfinished business. I didn't like this option because it was not only statistically unlikely, but also *incredibly* unfair.

Did they truly have no unfinished business? Or did they just *believe* that, and in reality, they were leaving their loved ones in the lurch. Like Grandma.

I had no way to test this because Mom was sticking with Grandma's rule that I could only Wake the elderly people who had died a natural or nontraumatic death. Any other cases were off limits until I was older.

So, option one could theoretically be the truth.

But then there was option two. That I wasn't trained

enough to use the power without Grandma there to guide me.

I *hated* that option.

It meant I might never be able to reach anyone's spark and I'd never help another person with their last wish. It would be the end of the family power.

I found myself wishing we knew other magical people so I'd at least have someone to talk it all through with.

"Kimmy?" Alex interrupted my thoughts. "What do you say?"

The only answer I had despite it all—try, try again.

"I'm coming." I followed Alex downstairs and he helped me get everything set up.

Mom had put her own rule in place that I wasn't allowed to Wake anyone without her or Alex present. She didn't trust me not to push like I had with Grandma.

She was probably right not to.

I stared down at Ms. Rosini and knew in my heart that this was going to go like every other time. I'd search and search and nothing would be there but the itchy sense that the spark was just out of reach. Like if I stretched that extra bit, I could grab it.

But I'd promised Mom and I'd promised Alex and I'd promised *Grandma* so I stuck to the limits and didn't push.

Picking up Ms. Rosini's hand, I went through all the steps—felt that same *tug, tug, tug* that kept haunting me every time I did this—and there was nothing.

"Nobody's home," I said to Alex as I gently repositioned Ms. Rosini.

He reached over to straighten her sleeve and replace the sheet. "I know it's been hard lately," he said. "But maybe she really is at peace. Maybe they all have been, and isn't that what everyone wants in the end?"

I loved Alex. I did. He'd become such an essential part of our family almost as soon as he and Mom started dating way back when. He'd fit right in with his humor and easy acceptance of the family power. He was as short and round as me and Mom, but with straight, dark brown hair and a warmer complexion. Alex was great.

But he wasn't the dad I needed to talk to about this.

"Yeah," I said, because agreeing was the easiest thing to do right now. "I'm going upstairs to read for a while before the visitation if that's okay?"

He shooed me off with a smile. "Come back down by two."

I put a few of the not-quite-special cookies on a plate on my way through the kitchen and headed up to my room. Shoving Morris aside so I had a little slice of bed to lie on, I got settled in and took Dad's journals out of my side table.

The last few months, I'd read them over and over again, hearing his voice clear in my brain. I could probably recite each one from heart by now.

Some of the page edges were getting a little soft, but the ink was clear and strong.

Flipping through, I found one of the entries that I'd read most often.

I've decided to start testing the cap.

I'll need to assess the limits before I can attempt to break through since the journals haven't been as helpful as I'd hoped.

The cap was an extreme solution to the problem. I think they put it on too soon. No one's ever had a chance to fully explore our powers. We know the furthest end of the spectrum, but what about all of the stages in-between?

Being able to Wake Dad for only a few minutes wasn't enough. I don't want to think about ~~when~~ if something happens to Mom or Julia.

There have to be more options.

What's possible in the middle ground?

I couldn't figure out half of what he was talking about. Dad knew all about the history of our power and what it was capable of. Whatever he knew made him want to try for more.

Grandma hadn't had a chance to share everything with me yet. She'd been so firm about the *process*. Trying to learn more on my own was slow going when I'd barely made a dent in the journals. Plus, they were all missing at least a few pages, just like Dad's. And despite looking everywhere, I hadn't been able to find any of Grandma's yet. It was beyond frustrating.

Clearly, there was something I was missing.

If the original form of the power was so strong and dangerous that it needed to be capped, what exactly were we capable of?

I shook my head, trying to dislodge those thoughts and ignoring the glare Morris sent me for disturbing him. That was a dangerous line of questioning.

Like that one Dad had tried to follow.

Going back to the beginning of the first journal, I found one of the entries that never failed to make me laugh. Capital letters filled the page in deep black slashes of ink.

ALL I WANT TO DO IS PLAY SOCCER WITH PAUL
BUT MOM IS MAKING ME SIT HERE AND BREATHE.

I loved picturing him sitting there being annoyed at Grandma as she made him practice. Before reading his journals, I'd never imagined him wanting to go do regular kid stuff. It made me wonder if there were things Grandma wanted to do instead of training when she was my age.

I should have asked.

Mom always made sure I got the regular kid stuff alongside the training. She'd even tried to get me to go to a summer camp this month with my two best friends, but I hadn't wanted to go that far from home. Not when I was the only person left to Wake people.

She and Alex still said to me before every Waking that it was my choice. I could use the power or not. I could take a break whenever I wanted.

Lately, there was a part of me that wanted to take a break. To be less of a failure for a little while. To be Kimmy Jones: totally normal kid.

So I tried it.

And it lasted five days.

Chapter Seven

I woke up with a gasp.

My room was quiet aside from the soft snores of Morris at the foot of my bed, but something had disturbed me.

A dream maybe?

Fumbling a hand over my side table, I grabbed my phone and squinted at the time. One a.m. on Wednesday morning. Gross. At least it was summer and I didn't have to worry about school. Flopping back against my pillows, I closed my eyes. Maybe I could manage to get another few—

Tug, tug, tug.

My eyes flew open as I sat up in shock at the twinge of my power in my chest. That had never happened when I wasn't trying to Wake someone. Was it normal? Was this another thing Grandma hadn't had time to teach me?

I lay there, wondering if it would stop on its own.

Tug, tug, tug.

"You know," I whispered, too sleepy to fall into panic mode yet. "I'm trying this new thing where I just do normal kid stuff and I've only been at it for a few days so if—"

Tug, tug, tug.

"Can it at least wait until the *sun* is up?"

. . . no response.

I took that as a yes. "Awesome," I muttered before pulling a pillow over my head and willing myself back to sleep.

Six hours later, I was less than rested. I'd kept waking up and fretting over what could be going on. I sat in bed, waiting, not even sure what I was hoping for.

A minute went by.

No tugs.

I scrubbed a hand over my face. Okay. That was good. It was for the best . . . right? Whatever happened during the night was a fluke. Back to normal kid time.

I was stupidly wide awake so I might as well get up. Throwing on some clothes, I headed out of my room to make my way downstairs. I could hear Mom and Alex in the kitchen talking in low voices and flashed back to the last time I walked in on them having a hushed conversation.

Giving my head a shake, I pushed back the tendrils of anxiety. They were probably having a quiet morning. The uninspiring gray sky visible through the window of the front door made hanging out in the kitchen over a cup of tea perfectly understandable. Except—

That *last* quiet morning was still so clear in my mind.

Slowing down as I reached the bottom steps, I tried to make out what they were saying.

"They have no idea what happened?" Mom asked softly. "But they must have suspicions if they're calling in extra help."

I halted completely. This sounded like *something*.

"That was Marco's guess," Alex replied.

Marco was one of Alex's friends, a paramedic. He always kept Alex up-to-date on what was going on in town so something must have happened last night.

"And they still haven't identified him?" Mom sighed. "His poor parents."

TUG, TUG, TUG.

"Whoa," I grunted as the force of the tugs pulled me forward and I stumbled down the last two steps, nearly tumbling to the floor.

"Kimmy?"

I straightened to see Mom and Alex peering at me from the kitchen table with matching concerned frowns. "You're up early," Alex said. "Sleep okay?"

"Not exactly," I said, dusting myself off before heading through the doorway to join them. "What's going on?"

"Oh, sweetie." Mom got up, gathering her dishes from the table and taking them to the sink. "It's nothing you have to worry about, okay?"

TUG, TUG, TUG.

The power disagreed with that.

"Did someone new come in last night or this morning?" What could be so special about them to cause my power to act out like this?

"Not yet," Alex said and Mom shot him a pointed look.

"But someone *did* pass away," I guessed.

Knots of agitation started to grow in my stomach at the next look they shared. We lived in and ran a funeral home so yeah, we dealt with death on a regular basis, but Mom and Alex—and Grandma—had always kept me away from the harder cases.

The ones where someone didn't die from old age.

. . . *tug, tug, tug.*

"What happened?" I asked again, quietly this time.

Alex looked to Mom with a defeated little shrug of his

shoulders. "She's going to find out soon enough," he said. "Better to hear it from us?"

Mom uncrossed her arms to swipe under her eyes and as I looked closer, I could see how red they were. She came back to the table, taking the seat next to me. "This is an in-house discussion," she said, using our term for keeping something a secret from the outside world. Usually that something was power-related, though.

"Someone died in the park last night," Mom said carefully. "They're not sure what happened or who he is, but they're investigating."

"Did someone hurt him?" There had to be more to this for how upset they both were.

"He was found by some high-school students who were in the park for the meteor shower last night and they saw a person running away," Alex said. He sighed. "So, yes, they are treating it as a suspicious death." He exchanged another look with Mom. A heavy one.

"What else aren't you telling me?" I demanded.

She cleared her throat and closed her eyes briefly before continuing. "He's young," Mom said. "It sounds like he's— he was about your age."

A kid.

My brain stuttered over the thought of it. A kid died

and they didn't know who he was or what happened to him. Possibly murdered. I rubbed at that spot in the center of my chest, the soreness there starting to blend with the ache in my heart for this stranger. A *kid*. Whatever happened to him, it wasn't fair.

It wasn't right.

Tug, tug, tug.

Mom wrapped an arm around my shoulders. "I know it's scary to think about and we're here if you want to talk."

"Yeah, it's just—that's really sad," I said, shaking my head and focusing back on our conversation. "Do you think I know him?" Basbridge was a small enough town to not be super exciting and yet large enough that not everyone knew everybody. I found myself hoping I didn't know him, but what if *no one* did? "What if they can't identify him?"

"They will." Mom sounded sure, but how could she be?

What if his case was never solved?

Tug, tug, tug!

She pressed a kiss to the top of my head and gave me a hug. "I have to get some things done in the office before our afternoon visitation. After breakfast, would you mind vacuuming the main viewing room for me?"

I nodded and she gave Alex a quick hug, too, before leaving the room.

Alex finished off his coffee and set the mug in the sink. "I'm going to inventory the prep room," he said, clasping my shoulder as he passed me on the way to the basement door. "We're both here, okay?"

"Okay."

Suddenly, I was alone in the kitchen. I got up with a sigh and poured myself a bowl of cereal. My thoughts kept circling back to the kid as I tried to eat.

What if they never figured out what happened to him? What if they couldn't find any clues? What if they were never able to find out who he was and he was left alone forever?

I could find out. I dropped my spoon on the table as the thought hit me and it was immediately followed up by a *tug, tug, tug* from my power.

There was no *way* that kid's spark wasn't still hanging around. He was the definition of unfinished business. I could Wake the boy and get some real answers that would actually help.

I shook my head. Snap out of it, Kimmy. That's a ridiculous idea. What was I going to do? Break into the hospital morgue?

TUGTUGTUG

"Okay, you don't get a vote when it's my butt on the

line," I said, ignoring the ridiculousness of talking to an empty room. "Let me think, please."

What did Grandma always say?

We don't intervene. We don't draw attention. We don't involve ourselves. Those were the rules. Important rules handed down through generations of Joneses for a reason.

If they didn't have any answers by the time he arrived at the funeral home—if he even came to ours—I could try Waking him then.

If his spark was still there. And if I could make the power work properly.

That was a lot of *ifs*.

I wished Grandma was here. She would absolutely tell me not to do it, but at least then I'd have a definite answer instead of thinking myself in circles.

For right now, there was only one thing I *could* do.

The vacuuming.

Using Grandma's preferred method of starting from the farthest wall and working my way back to the doors, I swept the machine back and forth. For a while the roar of the vacuum cleaner was enough to drown everything out. My own thoughts. The tugs. They were easier to ignore when I folded them into the rhythm of my movements. *Tug, tug, tug.* I pushed the machine forward. *Tug, tug, tug.* I pulled it back.

It was a little supernatural waltz.

I was halfway through the room before my distraction technique started to fail.

You could at least try, a little voice in my brain whispered at me.

Nope. No. I had no business getting involved in a police investigation. This was for the adults to handle.

He's all alone. You're carrying on with your chores like this is a normal day and that kid is all alone.

I shook my head and finished up the room at lightning speed. Wrapping the cord around the vacuum, I lugged it out into the hallway to put in back in the supply closet. As soon as I packed it away, the tugs went crazy.

TUGTUGTUG

It was like the power could sense I was only a few feet from the front door and if it pulled hard enough, it could yank me all the way to the hospital where that kid was waiting for me to help him. And somewhere else, his family was waiting, too. Except they didn't know they were waiting to say goodbye because they didn't even know what happened to him.

I groaned in frustration, spinning around and nearly running headlong into Tamsin.

We both jumped back in surprise.

"Kimmy!" She held one hand against her chest while she hastily shoved her phone into her back pocket. "You startled me."

"Sorry," I said, trying to edge my way past her. "Finishing up my chores. They're the worst, am I right?" I groaned again for emphasis.

Tamsin narrowed her eyes, focusing in on me with an unsettling intensity. "What's wrong?"

"Nothing," I said, failing to maintain anything close to a level volume. "Everything is fine and normal!" I ran up the stairs and into my room.

The tugs were quieter now, but still constant. I had to face facts. The power wanted me to act. *I* wanted to act.

Tug, tug, tug.

And something told me the power would work this time. I clapped my hands together once. Decision made. I had a morgue to break into.

Except I had no idea how to do that.

Chapter Eight

I grabbed my phone and opened up a new search tab.

What do you need to break into a morgue?

Moaning at the results, I tossed my phone back onto my bed. All the options were for breaking into the mortuary business which I didn't need help with, thanks. Where was a crime-centric search engine when you needed one?

My heart sped up a bit at that. Because this was a *crime* I was planning—even if it was for a good cause. I had to be extra prepared.

Gloves. Gloves would be good so I wouldn't leave any fingerprints. A disguise. A hat? Sunglasses? I could pull that off. Something to get the door open with? Basbridge wasn't exactly a bustling town and the hospital was kind of ancient, so the odds weren't too bad that it might even be unlocked. I should bring a crowbar just in case. Or maybe a crowbar was kind of intense.

A screwdriver? Yeah. That would be good.

What else?

Oh, a notebook to write down whatever the kid said. Then I could leave an anonymous note with his information for the authorities.

That was everything? Maybe?

Okay, wow. I was really doing this. All that was left was an excuse to give Mom and Alex as to why I was leaving the house. Something I hadn't done much of lately.

Impatient tugs prodded me to gather my supplies and stuff them into my backpack. Mom was still in the office so I headed there next to let her know I'd be going out.

Hovering outside the door, I tried to figure out how to start.

The thing was, I didn't lie to my parents that often. Or that successfully. Since we were already hiding this big secret from the rest of the world, being truthful with each other was extra important. Except, of course, Grandma Bev and Mom had kept an additional *huge* secret from me about Dad so maybe I could be forgiven for my own upcoming fib.

I took a deep, centering breath.

Then another.

How centered did one have to be to lie their face off?

One more breath. That should do it.

I stepped into the office, plastering a smile on my face as I approached the desk. "Hey, Mom!"

She looked up from her paperwork with a fond "Hey, hon."

"Is it okay if I go for a bike ride?" I asked, thinking on my feet.

"A bike ride?" Mom paused, her expression fighting a war between shocked and hopeful, which shouldn't have been a surprise considering how not interested I'd been in doing anything outside of the house for the past few months. "Where to?"

"The library and back." Lie.

"I don't know." Mom peered out the office window at the gray day. "They're calling for rain. Possibly even a storm. I don't want you to get caught in it."

"I'll be quick," I said.

Lie.

"I just want some fresh air," I added.

LIE!

I was getting good at this.

"Take your raincoat," Mom said, giving in, and I resisted

the urge to cheer. "And your phone! *And wear your helmet!*"
she called after me.

"Got it!" I yelled, grabbing my raincoat off the hook
and shoving it into my bag. I popped my helmet on, went
to lug my bike out of the garage, and hit the road.

The hospital was a bit farther than the library, plus
there was all of the sneaking around to do, so I had to
get a move on if I was going to sell the whole "short trip"
thing.

A few drops of rain splattered around me and the wind
picked up. I pedaled faster. Better to get out of sight before
Mom called me back in. Forward motion only.

Despite the rain getting heavier, I made it to the hospital
in record time and locked my bike up at the rack outside.

So far so good.

I took off my helmet and swapped it out for the ball cap and
sunglasses I'd stuffed in my bag. Slipping through the sliding
doors of the entrance, I meandered over to the directory on the
wall. Now was not the time to rush. I didn't want to draw any
scrutiny and get kicked out before I'd even had a chance to try.
Fortunately for me, the hospital wasn't all that busy midday on
a Wednesday. One person sat at the reception desk. There were
a couple more people in chairs by the front window, drinking
coffee. None of them looked my way.

Scanning the listings on the board, I tried to find the morgue—aha.

Basement level. Room B4.

I squared my shoulders and headed for the elevator to press the down button, tapping my toe as I waited. My luck held when the doors opened to reveal an empty inside. No one to question where I was going and no witnesses for what I was about to do.

With a ding, the doors opened at the basement level and I stepped off the elevator. The hallway ended in a T. I glanced at the sign on the wall, which said the morgue was off to the right. So far, *still* good. I crept down the hall past a few storage rooms and a bathroom, but had to stop short when I peeked around the corner.

A security guard stood at the door of the morgue.

I flung myself back. For all my preparations, I hadn't thought about having to deal with a *guard* at the door. My heart pounded in my chest as I tried to figure out what to do. Walk away?

TUG, TUG, TUG.

Bracing myself against the wall, I resisted the hard tugs urging me forward. *A moment to adjust, please and thanks,* I mentally objected. *I wasn't expecting to be faced with this level of security.*

What was my next move? Distract the guard and lure her away so I could sneak in?

The elevator dinged again. Someone else was coming and I was right in their path. White-hot panic buzzed through my brain as I looked for a place to hide.

The bathroom!

I ducked through the door on my right not a moment too soon. The elevator opened and footsteps came down the hall. Keeping the bathroom door open a tiny crack, I spotted a tall woman walking down the hall. She turned toward the morgue.

My plan also hadn't factored in it being such a popular place.

There was something familiar about that woman . . . oh! The new doctor, old Dr. Vernon's niece—what was her name? Dr. Wardwell. She'd taken over Dr. Vernon's practice when he passed away not long after Grandma died. He'd acted as the county coroner, too, so if she was taking on all of his old duties . . . she must be on her way to see the kid.

That was going to make things difficult.

The faint sounds of conversation drifted down the hall and I strained to hear. Sounded like she was convincing the guard to go for a coffee break since she was going to be there.

The guard passed by my hiding spot a moment later and there was a loud click as the stairwell door opened instead of the elevator. One down.

Now, how to get Dr. Wardwell to leave?

A pager went off, the chirp echoing through the hall, and I held my breath. There was no way I was this lucky. One second later, an announcement came over the crackly speaker, calling Dr. Wardwell to the Emergency Department.

I crossed my fingers—

Yes. Yes!

Dr. Wardwell rushed past me, grumbling under her breath as she went. The elevator dinged and then everything was quiet. I poked my head out into the hallway. Empty.

Okay. I was doing this.

Jogging around the corner to the morgue, I hoped my luck would hold out a little while longer. A quick test of the door proved otherwise. Locked.

I dug the screwdriver out of my bag and examined the door handle, pretending I had a clue what I was doing. It was round with the lock right in the center. People did this in movies all the time. How hard could it be?

Gripping the screwdriver firmly, I gave it a little shake. "Don't let me down." I jammed the tip into the lock and wiggled it around as I twisted the handle.

After a few minutes of no give, I was beginning to think the movies had lied to me. "Come on," I grunted, jiggling the screwdriver. "This. Has. To. Work!"

The door popped open.

"Thank you!" I slipped inside the room, patting the door as I shut it behind me.

The main lights were off in the morgue, but light came in from the hallway through the window in the door and a little lamp was shining on one of the desks. It was enough for me to work in. I didn't want to turn everything on and risk alerting anyone walking by to my presence.

Pulling off the sunglasses and hat, I stuffed them into my bag. Better.

A rumble of thunder rolled overhead and through the windows near the ceiling I could see the rain pouring down. Not good. Mom would be calling any minute, wondering where I was and wanting to come pick me up. Maybe I could buy myself some extra time.

I grabbed my phone and shot off a quick text, letting her know I'd arrived at the library and was going to wait out the storm there.

That should help, but I still had to work fast.

First step was to find the kid. There were three tables in the morgue and only one had a body bag on it. Even if it wasn't labeled John Doe, I'd have a hunch this was the right one based on how dramatic the tugs in my chest had gotten. They were pulsing in time with my heartbeat at this point.

I took a deep breath and stepped toward the table, staring down at the body bag. Last chance. No going back after this. Could I really go through with it?

The tugs grew quiet and I reached out with a shaky hand. Unzipping the bag, I stared down at the person inside.

It was a kid.

I *knew* it would be a kid, but knowing wasn't the same as seeing—not when I was staring down at someone my own age.

I didn't recognize him. He must have gone to one of the schools on the other side of town. I couldn't decide if not knowing him was better or worse.

He was frowning a little and his blond hair was all tangled on one side. A smudge of dirt streaked across his pale cheek. My fingers itched to wipe it off until I remembered it was evidence. Clues to who he was and what had happened.

Clues that might—or might not—lead to answers.

I could get answers for sure.

The last of my doubts faded away.

Time to see if he'd Wake.

Chapter Nine

I didn't want the boy to freak out when he Woke, so I unzipped the bag the rest of the way and pulled the sides down as much as I could.

There were smudges of dirt on his clothes as well and doodles along the sides of his sneakers. Little planets and stars. Cute. Grandma would've flipped if I'd done that. I could practically hear the lecture. *It's footwear, Kimmy, not a sketchpad.*

I'd take the scolding if it meant she was here.

My phone dinged with a text, startling me as it echoed in the quiet of the morgue. I grabbed it out of my bag as quickly as I could and silenced it. Not like it was going to disturb anyone in here, but better safe than sorry. Anyone could be walking by.

One glance at the screen had me shoving it away and straightening up. I needed to hurry or Mom was going to hunt me down.

Time to focus.

Carefully taking the boy's hand in between mine, I took a deep breath. Here we go. The *tug, tug, tug* picked up again as I connected to my power and let the energy flow through me.

When I closed my eyes, I pictured the power surging from my hands to his, running free to search out his spark. His spark which was . . .

Not there.

"No!" I cried out, squeezing his hand tighter. This was impossible. There was *no way* he didn't have a spark hanging around. It was here somewhere and I was going to find it.

I had to.

I reached as far as I could. The physical space inside of a person was finite, but the part that Grandma called the metaphysical space was much bigger.

In the past, a spark had either been right there or it hadn't. I'd never had to search too far—not until I'd tried to Wake Grandma. Mom had stopped me then and I'd stopped myself with everyone else since.

There was no stopping this time.

Taking another long, slow, deep breath, I sent the power out further, putting all of my energy into this one goal. *Find his spark.*

Reaching, reaching, reaching until I hit a wall of resistance.

No. No, no, no.

Tug, tug, tug.

No stopping.

There was a tickle in my nose and I sniffed a few times, remembering the nosebleed from last time. I ignored it.

TUG, TUG, TUG.

I pushed harder.

My head started to spin and I pushed *through*.

A burst of light poked at my eyelids and I cracked them open, hoping someone hadn't come into the room and flicked on the overheads. My heart was pounding and it took me a moment to process what I was seeing. Then my eyes flew wide open.

The good news was that no one had come into the room.

The *incredibly weird* news was that my hands were glowing.

That bright golden light I always pictured when I used my power was radiating from my hands and spreading out to the kid in front of me.

Nothing from Grandma's training or Dad's journals had brought up the possibility of *actual glowing hands*.

"Ummmm, what do I do here," I whispered. This was completely new territory. The urge to flap my hands around and try to shake the glow off was strong, but a gentle *tug, tug, tug* held me in place. Like a reassurance that I was on the right track.

I'd take it. I could figure out the hows and whys later, but right now, I was going to keep going. Closing my eyes, I ignored the headache that was now a dull roar and took a few more deep, centering breaths before reaching out with my power again.

It stretched until my connection with the boy was as narrow as a thread. One that could snap if I wasn't careful.

All of a sudden, at the edge of my reach, there it was.

An energy that *belonged* with this kid. His spark.

I let my power spool around it and pulled, but it wouldn't budge. "I've come this far," I gritted out, every muscle in my body tense with effort. "Do *not* mess with me." With one more yank, I had it. And I didn't know what to make of it.

The boy's spark wasn't like any I'd come across before. Sparks were usually warm, and bright, and relatively calm despite their unfinished business. The boy's spark was bright, but it was smaller than usual, with torn edges. Cold streaks of blue cut through the warmth and its energy was chaotic. Trying to anchor it in place was like trying to wrangle an angry cat.

I finally managed it; my power wrapped tight around the spark.

Thunder shook the room.

The boy Woke with a gasp.

"Hey, hey," I said quietly, holding his hand tightly as his eyes darted around. They finally landed on me and I tried to give him a friendly smile. "You're okay. Try to take a few slow breaths. Slower." I breathed in and out with him until his evened out.

He looked around the room before his gaze returned to me. "Wha—what's going on?" he asked. "Where am I?"

Now I was torn because I didn't want to lie, but I was also pretty sure that telling him the truth would only freak him out. "You're in the hospital," I said, hoping that was truthful enough. "Can you tell me your name?"

"Devon," he said. "Devon Sawyer."

The tight knot that had been sitting in my stomach started to loosen. Even if I learned nothing else, I had a name. Something we could use to track down his family.

"Nice to meet you, Devon," I said. "My name's Kimmy."

"Hi," Devon said, looking around distractedly. "This doesn't look like a hospital room."

"It's a waiting area," I said, trying to whip up a cover story on the fly. "They need to take you for some scans."

He squinted at me. "You're a kid," he said. "Why are *you* here?"

"I'm a volunteer. I keep people company when they have to wait for stuff like this." What I really needed to do was steer this conversation so he'd stop asking questions and I could get more answers. "What's the last thing you remember?"

"I was at the park," he said, eyes going unfocused. "I wanted to see something . . . the meteor shower . . ."

Meteor shower. I'd heard Alex talking about that yesterday, but it was at two o'clock in the morning or something.

"I couldn't see it from my room," Devon continued. "So I snuck out. I remember looking up and there was this blue light and . . ." He shook his head. "That's all."

Not a lot to go on. "Did you see anyone?" I pressed and Devon's face scrunched up.

"I—I don't know," he said, voice hitching as fear crept into it. "Everything's blank. I don't remember."

I opened my mouth to answer when a huge burst of lightning lit up the sky. The room went dark. I jumped, pulling my hand away from Devon, and then cursed myself for doing so. The abrupt loss of connection wouldn't have been nice for him.

Should I leave him be? Hope that he can find some peace? Or try to Wake him again and see if I could help him remember more details to piece together what happened? That was *if* I could even manage to Wake him a second time.

Thunder rumbled and I sighed. My head was aching and the rest of me had its fair share of complaints. Maybe the power outage was a sign that I'd pushed my luck far enough and it was time to leave. I should find my phone, use the flashlight to put everything back how I'd found it, and get out of here.

I reached for my bag.

Then, through the shadows, a voice called out. "Are you still there?"

Chapter Ten

I was not proud of the fact that I screamed.

But I did. Loudly.

And the absolutely-should-not-still-be-alive kid screamed back.

Reaching out with the power, I ran smack into the connection humming vibrantly between us. Which was impossible. It should have broken as soon as we stopped touching. I visualized the connection like Grandma taught me and tried to dissolve it. Snap it. Anything. But it wouldn't budge.

"What is *happening?*" I could barely hear myself over my pulse pounding in my ears.

"I don't know!" Devon yelled.

The emergency lights clicked on, flickering overhead, and now I could see him again. He'd sat up on the tray, letting his legs dangle over the side as he stared at me.

"How are you still alive?" I cried.

"What?" Devon reared back. "Am I supposed to be dead?"

Oh, crap. "Uh . . ."

"Am I *supposed to be dead*?" he demanded.

"Kind of?" I blurted out and he looked at me like I had two heads, which was probably a fair reaction. "Gimme a minute and I'll try to explain." Somehow.

This was bad. This was *beyond* bad.

I paced a bit, eyeing Devon until he made a little "Well?" gesture at me. He deserved some answers. Hopefully he could handle them.

"Okay," I said, stopping in front of him with my arms crossed as I braced myself for his reaction. "Here's the situation. You died in the park. No one knows how. My family has the power to bring people back from the dead temporarily so I decided to come here and Wake you to see if I could get some answers so you could be properly laid to rest. But something's gone wrong because the connection should have broken when I let go of your hand. You shouldn't have . . . stayed Awake."

Devon narrowed his eyes at me. After a beat, he shook

his head and started chuckling. "Sure." He laughed. "This is some kind of prank, right? There's hidden cameras?" He started looking around the room.

"No! It's—" I huffed. We didn't have time for this. Dr. Wardwell or the guard or *anybody* could walk in any minute. "Look around you. We're in the morgue. That's a *body bag* you're sitting on. That wall is full of refrigeration units for storing dead bodies. How do you explain waking up here? You *died*, okay?"

"Oh." Devon looked down and ran a hand over the material of the bag, thinking things over. "Maybe I'm dreaming?" he murmured. "Pretty strange freaking dream."

He reached out and *pinched* my arm.

"Ow!" I rubbed at the spot. "Why?"

Devon shrugged at me. "That's how you check to see if you're dreaming."

"No! You pinch yourself. *You pinch yourself!*" I reached out and pinched him back.

"Ow!"

"Yeah. Not nice, is it?"

He glared at me, rubbing his own arm and I took a moment to calm down and remind myself that I was a professional. "Look," I said. "I realize this is scary and you probably have a lot of questions—"

Devon snorted at that.

"But if you come with me," I forged ahead, "I will do my best to answer them and figure this whole thing out."

"Figure this whole thing out?" he scoffed. "As in, figure out how to make me dead again? That's what you're worried about, right?"

Yes. Probably shouldn't say that, though.

"I was thinking more like what happened to you," I said. "Why don't we start with that?"

"Why do I have to go with you? Why can't I go home and you let me know what you find out?" Devon brushed at a spot of dirt on his pants. "I don't see why you need me."

"Because you *died*."

"But I'm *fine*," he shot back.

"People saw you . . . like that," I said, trying to figure out how to make him understand. "If they see you walking around later, they're going to have questions. Really difficult questions."

"Sounds like a you problem," Devon grumbled.

"Okay, truth? I don't know how permanent you being alive again actually is," I admitted and Devon looked up at me sharply. "Yeah, so do you want to risk traumatizing your family or could you give me a bit of time?"

He stared at his shoes, chewing on his lip. Ducking my

head down, I caught his eye. "Will you *please* come with me? For now?"

Devon eventually nodded slowly.

"Yes? Great. Come on," I said, waving him forward. "We need to get out of here before anyone shows up."

He hopped off the table as I grabbed my bag and pulled out my phone, wincing at the *many* texts from Mom as I pressed the flashlight icon. One problem at a time.

Exits, exits, exits. Taking the stairs back up to the lobby risked us running into the guard, and I should really avoid being seen leaving with a resident of the morgue.

Former resident now, I supposed.

Focus, Kimmy.

An emergency exit might set off an alarm and I didn't want to chance that.

"Didn't you say we should leave?" Devon piped up.

"Yes," I said, shushing him. "I'm trying to decide how."

He wandered over to the other side of the room and pointed up at the large rectangular windows near the ceiling. "Do those open?"

After climbing up onto a desk and then a large filing cabinet, it turned out that, yes, the windows did open. And because we were in the basement, they opened up on the ground level.

I threw my backpack and helmet out ahead of us, let Devon crawl through, and then I followed. By the time we made it out, we were both soaked, but at least we were free.

"Come on." I gestured for him to follow and we walked around to the front of the hospital to get my bike. The sky had a spooky greenish tone to it and there was a strange haze in the air, but the rain was starting to let up and I hadn't heard any thunder for a while. Things could be worse—

"Wait." I flung my arm out to stop Devon and maneuvered us behind a bush.

"What—"

"Shhhh!" I tried to peek through the foliage.

Tamsin was walking up to the front entrance of the hospital. She slowed down when she caught sight of my bike and her head swivelled as she looked around.

"No, no, no," I whispered.

Had Mom sent her out to look for me? I doubted that was part of her job description. Maybe it was a coincidence. I mentally willed her to keep moving, breathing a sigh of relief when she finally went inside.

"Who were we hiding from?" Devon's voice popped up directly next to my ear and I nearly fell over.

"No one," I said, shoving him away from where he was

trying to peer over my shoulder. "Come on, let's go."

We jogged up to my bike and I unlocked it. Since I only had the one helmet, we walked—me wheeling the bike down the sidewalk at a brisk pace while trying not to run over Devon who was zigzagging around me.

"So, I was dead," he said and I flapped a hand at him.

"Ease up on the D-word when we're out in public," I begged.

He rolled his eyes. "But I *was*," he said. "And now I'm not. That's like straight out of a comic book." Devon stopped in his tracks. "Does this mean I'll get superpowers, too?"

"What? No." Ugh, I *really* hoped not. One surprise at a time. "Also, I do not have *superpowers*," I hissed, waving him forward. "And you're only allowed to ask questions if you keep walking."

"Did you or did you not bring me back to life?" he asked, finally moving again.

"I have *one* very specific power," I allowed. "It's a family thing."

That opened the floodgates. He asked question after question about how the power worked, who in my family had it, how did we "wield" it, why didn't I know what wield meant, and on and on.

I pushed back my annoyance and answered everything

as best I could. Questions were a good distraction. He was taking this whole thing very well. Disturbingly well, so I'd keep answering questions if that was keeping a possible meltdown at bay.

We were almost home when he asked one that caught me off guard.

"Where does it come from?"

I sent him a side-eyed look. "What do you mean?"

Devon shrugged at me. "What powers the power? Is it a mutation like in comics or—"

"It's not—I mean maybe—" Grandma had always explained it as something that came with being a Jones. She made it sound simple. I should have asked more questions when I could.

"It's just something my family's been able to do for a long time now," I said.

That earned me a crinkled-up nose. "There has to be a catch." He didn't meet my eyes, kicking a rock as he walked down the sidewalk with his hands shoved in his pockets. "In all the books I've read, when someone uses magic like that," Devon said, "there's always a catch or a price to pay. What's yours?"

Struck by that thought, I stopped short and it took him a couple of steps to notice before he reversed course and came back. My hands were white-knuckled on the handlebars.

Grandma never mentioned a catch, but she'd talked a lot about the limitations of our power and the cap that had been put on it. *And* the people we Woke always went back to rest.

"Kimmy?" Devon was watching me carefully.

"No catch," I said, trying to keep my concern off my face. "We use the power to help people, not for our own gain, and we keep it a secret. We're all good."

But were we? I'd broken the cap and Devon was still here. What was the catch, I wondered, when someone stayed alive? I watched him shrug at my answer and continue down the sidewalk. Was something going to happen?

We walked along in silence for a bit until—

"Has anyone you've brought back ever turned into a zombie?"

"Seriously?"

"It's a reasonable question."

Five minutes and three more zombie questions later, we arrived at my house. Devon stared at the sign. "You live in a funeral home?"

"Yup."

His eyebrows crawled up his forehead. "And you bring dead people back to *life*?"

"I told you!" I flung a hand in the air. "It's not usually permanent!"

"Terrible business model," he muttered.

The rain chose that moment to pick up again and I took the opportunity to hustle us into the garage. After stashing my bike, I brought Devon around to the backyard where there was a back entrance that led into the kitchen. Hopefully by using that we could avoid running into my mom or Alex and their inevitable questions about my guest.

My very not-dead dead guest.

Two steps from the door, a huge lightning strike lit up the sky so bright, it made Devon's eyes look like they were glowing blue. We both flinched back against the force of it. A heavy gust of wind followed that tried to suck the air right out of me as it passed by.

"Come on," I called to him as I staggered over to open the door. "Get inside." The quiet warmth of the kitchen helped settle me enough to start thinking of an actual plan. "We have to get you upstairs and out of sight," I said. "If my parents see you, they'll kill me."

"Couldn't you just bring yourself back?" Devon asked with a crooked little grin.

"Hilarious." I levelled a flat look at him as I herded him through the kitchen. "This way."

"Whoa, your house is so cool," he breathed, looking at the fancy woodwork in the hallway leading to the staircase.

I hushed him and hurried him along.

"It looks fancy."

"*Shhhh.*"

"Do you ever slide down this banister?"

"Please. Stop. Talking."

We were halfway up the stairs when my mom called out from her office. "Kimmy? Is that you?"

"Go, go!" I whispered to Devon, pushing him forward. "My room is the last one on the left. Close the door and stay there—and *be quiet!*"

"Okay, all right already, calm down." He brushed away my hands, but managed to be out of sight before Mom came into the hallway.

"Kimmy!" she exclaimed, hurrying over to me. "Where have you been? Look at you, you're soaked. Why didn't you answer your phone? Alex went out to find you so he could give you a ride home. You rode your bike in this weather? That's so dangerous! And you're leaving puddles all over the floor. You're lucky you didn't get struck by lightning, honestly—"

"Mom." I broke through the rant. "You're right. I'm sorry. I thought the storm was over and it was safe to head home." Grimacing, I gestured to my semi-soaked clothes. "I was wrong."

She sighed and ran a hand over my damp hair. "It's not like you, sweetie," Mom said. "You had us really worried."

"I didn't mean to," I said as I leaned in for a hug. She put a hand out to gently stop me.

"Maybe you should get dried off and changed first." Mom laughed. "I'll text Alex and let him know you made it home."

"Tell him I'm sorry, please! Tamsin as well."

"Tamsin?" Mom looked confused.

"You didn't send her to look for me, too?" I asked, thinking about seeing her at the hospital.

"That's not exactly in her job description," Mom said, shaking her head. "She said she had an errand to run. Although what it could be in this weather, I don't know."

Hunh. I guess it *had* been a coincidence. I headed for the stairs.

"Kimmy!"

Freezing in place, I turned slowly at Mom's call.

"You don't ignore us when we call or text," she said. "You know that's the rules for having a phone so there have to be consequences. You're grounded for a week. No phone and no leaving the house."

Considering the fact that I'd just kidnapped a not-dead corpse from the morgue, I didn't think laying low would be a problem. "That's fair," I said, handing over my phone before jogging up the stairs and dashing into my room.

Devon jumped at my sudden arrival, a guilty look flitting across his face. Then I noticed the open drawer of the bedside table. And the familiar journal in his hands.

"What are you doing? Were you snooping?" I demanded as I stalked forward to snatch my journal out of his grasp and stuff it back into the drawer. "This is private. Don't touch."

"Sorry." Devon did look at least a little bit sorry as he retreated. "I got bored. And nosy. Wanted to see what kind of stuff a person with magical powers keeps in her room." He scratched at the back of his neck. "My bad."

"Did you read it?" I asked and he shook his head. "Good," I said. "Don't."

The room was thick with tension and I gave myself a shake. There were bigger things to worry about. Time to focus. I clapped my hands together. "First things first, we need to get into dry clothes." Devon was a bit taller than me, but we looked to be close to the same size otherwise. I dug through my drawers and found him a pair of sweatpants, a baggy T-shirt, and some socks, grabbing an outfit for myself while I was at it.

I left him to change in my room while I changed in the bathroom, hanging my wet clothes over the shower curtain. My mind was spinning as I tried to figure out what to tackle next.

I had no idea why my power had kept Devon alive or how long it would last, but there was an equally pressing problem: he was now missing from the morgue.

Someone was going to notice that at some point and start looking for him. What if—I smacked a hand against my forehead when I realized I'd forgotten to put on my gloves in the morgue. I'd left prints everywhere. And I hadn't checked for cameras. I could be on the security footage! How long until they traced it all back to me?

And! We still had no idea what had happened to Devon in the first place! The whole reason I went there to Wake him. All we had to go on was a blue light.

One thing at a time.

I could work with Devon to see if we could shake

any more memories loose. Then I could subtly check in with Mom and Alex to find out if they'd heard anything about the morgue escape. Maybe take a peek online for any news.

In terms of finding answers about what was going on with the power, I really only had one place to look: the Jones family journals.

Chapter Eleven

Grandma and Dad weren't here and Mom and Alex didn't know anything more than I did, which meant the journals were the only resource I had left. I needed to read through as much as I could as quickly as I could—even if that meant sharing them with a non-Jones.

A really annoying non-Jones.

Leaving the bathroom, I snuck down the hall to Grandma's room, slipped inside, and shut the door behind me.

Everything was exactly as Grandma had left it.

Mom asked me once about cleaning some things out, but I'd had a slight meltdown and she hadn't brought it up again. I liked it better this way. It let me almost believe she was coming back any minute. I'd only been in a few times to take a new journal to read or return one, and each time I'd rushed in and out, feeling like an intruder in her space.

Looking around now, I realized how dusty it had become. She would have been so annoyed by that. I trailed a hand over her dresser and picked up a photo. It was one of the two of us from when I was a little kid. I was sitting on her lap in the big green armchair while she read to me. Grabbing a corner of my shirt, I carefully wiped off the dust.

That was better.

I set it down on the dresser and made a mental note to come back for a proper clean after I got things with Devon sorted. Open the windows and get some fresh air in here for her.

Stepping over to the bookshelf that held the journals, I pursed my lips as I looked it over. The thing was jam-packed. That was a whole lot of words we were going to have to slog through and not a lot of time to do it. What was the best way to tackle this?

I squinted at the rows of leather-bound spines. Grandma had them in chronological order so I grabbed a few from the beginning, middle, and end, hoping to give us a broad historical spectrum to work with. Stacking them in my arms, I tiptoed back across the hall.

Devon was sitting on my bed when I returned to my

room, changed into his borrowed outfit with his wet clothes hanging over my closet door.

He waved his hands in the air at me. "Didn't touch a thing!"

"If I had a gold star, I'd give it to you," I said, setting the journals down beside him. I swatted his hand away when he reached for the top one. "Rules first."

He rolled his eyes, but sat back to listen.

"These are priceless documents that can never be replaced," I said. "The Jones family history is meant to be read only by members of the Jones family. I will allow you access to them, but you have to swear that you will be the most careful with them that you have ever been with any item in your whole life."

Devon nodded and I stared at him, waiting.

"Oh!" he said, understanding flooding his face. "You want me to actually say it. Okay. Yes, I swear I will be the most careful with them."

"That you have ever been . . ." I prompted.

"That I have ever been with any item in my whole life. Cross my heart," he added.

"You better." I handed him half and sat down beside him. "So, we need to figure out what's going on with the power and—"

"I thought you were going to figure out what happened to me?" Devon interrupted with a pout.

"I am," I said, hopping up to grab us paper and pens as well. "But part of what's happened to you is because of my power malfunctioning. And this is something we can do right now that won't draw any attention."

Devon made a face at the journals in his hands. "I died," he said. "I shouldn't be getting homework."

"I brought you back to life, remember? So quit complaining." I settled back down and opened the first journal in my pile, elbowing him until he did the same.

"What are we looking for?" he asked, riffling through the pages.

"Anything that talks about what the power specifically does or about people staying Awake," I said, concentrating on trying to decipher the spidery handwriting on the page in front of me.

Devon grumbled a bit more, but he dove in and for a while the only sound was turning pages. I made a note of anything that could be helpful, but there was nothing about the connection holding without touch or people *staying* alive.

The Jones behind the journal I was reading, Abigail, talked about her father stressing the importance of being mindful of her own spark. No further details, though. I almost put it down and headed back to Grandma's room so I could try one more time to find *her* journals. Like this time would be any different from all the other times I'd searched.

Not that I had any guarantee she'd have more information in her journals than the ones we were currently reading, but I wanted the comfort of *her* words. Her thoughts. Something I'd been missing every day for the past few months.

Devon made a surprised noise beside me.

"What?" I craned my head to peek at the page he was reading.

"Says here Tobias Jones made six zombies," he said. The rest of his words were lost when I chucked a pillow at his face and he gasped. "Be careful of the journals!"

"Focus," I growled.

We kept reading for the next few hours until Mom called for me to help with dinner.

"Oh, right, food," Devon said, looking down at his stomach and poking it. "I'm hungry. Can dead people get hungry? Should we be worried? I'm not craving brains yet so that's good."

"We've been over this," I said. "You're not *dead* dead." I wasn't one hundred percent sure how alive he was, but he definitely wasn't dead. "Plus, you weren't embalmed or autopsied yet—"

"*Gross.*"

"Which means your insides are all intact. I don't see why you wouldn't be hungry. The problem is—"

"I can't go downstairs," he finished glumly.

"We can't risk Mom and Alex seeing you." I nodded. "But I'll sneak some food up to you later, okay?"

"I hate being not *dead* dead." Devon flopped face-first onto my bed.

"I'll bring cookies, too," I promised and he raised a thumbs-up into the air as I left.

I thumped my way down the stairs and nearly ran into Tamsin on my way to the kitchen.

"Oops, careful there!" She ducked neatly out of my way and turned to smile at me. "I'm headed home—" Tamsin did a double take, eyes going wide once she was finally facing me. "What, uh, what have you been up to today, Kimmy?"

She kept staring at me with a strained, frozen smile on her face and it was impossible—there was no way—but I had a horrible hunch that she knew *exactly* what I'd been up to today.

"Went for a bike ride to the library," I said, inching my way past her.

"Cool," Tamsin said. "Cool, cool, cool. Um. Maybe we should—"

"Kimmy!" Mom called again before appearing in the doorway. "There you are—oh, Tamsin, you're leaving? Thank you for your help today. Don't know what we'd do without you."

"My pleasure, Julia," Tamsin said, stiff smile still plastered across her face. "I'll see you tomorrow." She nodded her head jerkily at the both of us before hustling out the front door.

I might not know Tamsin very well yet, but I knew her well enough to know that was weird. And I was dealing with a little bit too much weirdness already so any extra was—oh, Mom was talking to me again.

"—are you listening?" She pressed a hand against my forehead. "Did you get chilled in the rain? You're a bit out of it, sweetie."

"Sorry." I shook my head. "I think I'm tired from my ride. You said you wanted help with dinner?"

"Yes, please." Mom wrapped an arm around my shoulders and kissed the top of my head before guiding me into the kitchen. Alex was already at the counter prepping vegetables.

He paused in his chopping and shot a grin at me. "The adventurer returns," he declared. "Did you have a nice bike ride through the gale-force winds?"

"Yes?" He laughed at my sheepish smile. "I really am sorry," I said.

"She's promised it won't happen again," Mom said, handing me plates. "And I'll be double-checking the volume control on her phone when she gets her privileges back."

We settled into our routine of getting dinner ready. Mom and Alex told me about their day as they finished making the spaghetti and the salad, and I set the table.

Once we were seated, I tried to figure out how to work Devon into the conversation to see if they'd heard anything. Mom was the one to give me an opening.

"I could not believe how strange that storm was today," she said. "Pouring buckets one minute, clear the next, and then starting all over again."

"It was pretty strong," I said. "Do you think they'll still be able to gather evidence from the park?"

Mom paused with her fork halfway to her mouth. "Evidence?"

"From the boy they found there last night," I said, not sure where the confusion was coming from. "Or this morning, I guess. Has there been any news? Do they know who he is?"

Alex blinked at me. "What boy?"

What boy? *What boy?* "The boy they found in the park! He died and no one knows how or who he is?" I sat back in my seat as Mom and Alex exchanged concerned looks. How did they not remember this?

"Do I need to check your viewing history?" Mom asked, setting her fork down carefully and levelling a stare at me. "Have you been watching scary movies or one of those murder documentary things? If you're watching shows that are giving you nightmares—"

"No! No, I—" I had no idea what kind of explanation to give. I couldn't get into the whole story since they clearly remembered *none* of it and it would open up the door to way more questions than I had time to answer. "I saw something on the news and I guess I got mixed up and thought they were talking about someplace around here."

"Nothing like that has happened in Basbridge," Mom said with an air of finality.

"Good to know." I turned to Alex, seriously needing to get a change of topic going. "Did you do something different with the sauce this time? I'm tasting a little tang."

Alex's eyes lit up and he started in on his latest culinary experiments, providing an excellent distraction for Mom. I listened and nodded at all the right places, but I kept turning this new piece of the puzzle over in my mind, unable to make anything fit together.

After dinner, I volunteered to do the dishes and used the time alone in the kitchen to put together a meal and some snacks for Devon. A sandwich—because there was no way I trusted him to eat spaghetti in my room—some carrot sticks, granola bars, an apple, and the promised cookies. A couple from batch number twenty. That should be good. I had enough room left on the tray for a water bottle and some napkins. Well stocked, I headed back upstairs.

I took a detour to the living room where Mom and Alex were watching a show and set the tray down on the floor in the hallway before poking my head inside. "I'm a little tired from my storm adventure," I said. "I'm gonna go read for the rest of the night."

It almost backfired when Mom wanted to take my temperature, but I made a narrow escape by convincing her all I needed was some quiet time.

Even though I knew I was about to get the opposite of that.

"Finally." Devon heaved out a sigh when I came through the door. "That took forever. I'm starving. You have nothing to eat in here. I checked. Yes, that's right. I snooped some more. Because I was dying. Again."

"I'm sorry, here." I carefully set the tray down on my side table for him to sort through. "Brought you a bit of everything."

He dove right in, starting with the cookies. "Mmm." He hummed a happy little munching sound. "These aren't bad. Missing a little something, though."

I closed my eyes and poked at the connection. Maybe I could break it *now*.

. . . nope.

Sighing, I opened my eyes to shoot him a glare that went right over his head as he started in on the next cookie. "At least eat over the tray," I grumbled.

He leaned over it dutifully and I dove into the latest update. "So, my parents have no memory of telling me about you being found in the park. I brought it up at dinner and they thought I was talking about a show or something."

"What?" Devon coughed, choking on his mouthful. I made sure he could breathe before handing him the water bottle.

"Yeah, I have no idea why," I said. "But it has to be connected. The question is: are they the only ones? Or has everyone forgotten about you?"

"Not everyone," he said, pointing at me.

True. Why did *I* still remember?

Thank goodness Mom had forgotten to confiscate a certain *other* electronic device I had at my disposal. I dug out my tablet while Devon continued eating and started searching for any information I could find. It had been hours since he was found. Somebody had to have picked up the story. I searched every news site I could think of from local ones to national and checked as many social media sites as I could. Even looked through a few local chat groups.

Nothing. Not one single line.

It was like it had never happened.

"Well," I said to Devon as he crunched his way through the carrots. "The good news is, I don't think anyone is going to be hunting us down for breaking you out of the morgue."

He tilted his head at me for that. "Does it count as breaking me out when it was because I was alive again? Isn't it more like releasing me back into the wild?"

"That will be our defense if anyone does come looking." I laughed.

Devon's own laughter faded after a bit, face turning serious. "Why do you think no one but you remembers me? Do you think it's just the memory of finding me that's gone? Or do you think it's all of me? Like—like I've been erased."

I hadn't even thought of that possibility. "I'll check." I picked up my tablet again and searched "Devon Sawyer, Basbridge."

No results.

"That doesn't necessarily mean anything." I tried to reassure him when his face fell as he saw the screen. "Lots of kids don't show up in searches if they're not on social media or in the news."

"So, how do we find out for sure?"

"I don't know," I admitted. We'd have to be very careful about it. "I'm adding it to the list of things that need answering."

"Awesome." He poked at the crumbs on his plate.

"Hey," I said, waiting for him to meet my gaze again. "We're going to figure this out. I promise."

He finally nodded, some of the tension bleeding out of his shoulders. "Let me guess," he said, covering a sniff. "We've got to keep reading in order to do that?"

"Ding, ding!" I held up my hand for a high five. "Got it in one."

"I'm not high-fiving that." Devon shook his head.

"See if I bring you more cookies," I muttered and he quickly smacked my hand before I could lower it.

Okay. Go team.

✳ ✳ ✳

We got a few hours of reading in before there was a knock on the door and I realized it was bedtime. "Stay down," I hissed at Devon as I swiftly kicked him off the bed so he'd land out of sight. Ignoring his indignant cry, I leapt up to meet Mom as she cracked open the door.

"Hey, hon—oh, hi, there you are," she said, startled by my sudden appearance in the doorway. "Checking in and saying good night."

"Night, Mom," I said, giving her a hug. "Love you."

"Love you, too." She squeezed me back. "Try to clean up some of those journals so you have room to sleep, okay?" She laughed.

"Will do." I closed the door and leaned against it with a sigh.

Devon popped his head up from the other side of the bed. "That was *rude*."

"Excuse me for being a quick thinker." I snorted. Mom finding him in my room was a mess that we did not have time to deal with. "Let's pack this up," I said, ignoring his grumbles. "We'll do better with fresh eyes in the morning."

I set up a little bed for Devon on the floor that he declared "fine" and we both settled down to sleep. It was quiet in the darkness of my room for about two minutes.

"Hey, Kimmy?"

"Yes, Devon."

"You know that last-wish thing you were telling me about?" he whispered. "The one your family does when you bring people back?"

"Yeah?" I said, bracing myself for another round of twenty thousand questions.

"Is that what you were going to do for me?"

Part of me wanted to turn the side table lamp on so I could see him, but the other part suspected this conversation was only happening because we were in the dark.

"I would have," I said. "I wanted to find out who you were and what happened to you so your family would have some answers, but I would have asked what your last wish was, too. If you wanted to send a message or something."

Devon let out a little "hmm" at that.

There was silence for a few minutes and I thought maybe that was that until—

"What would you say?" he asked quietly.

"What?"

"If you were going to send a message as a—a last wish," Devon clarified.

"I have an elaborate scavenger hunt planned so whoever

is left behind will be entertained in my absence," I said.

"Seriously?"

"No."

Devon groaned. "That would actually be so cool, though," he said. "For real, what would you say?"

"Honestly, I haven't thought about it that much," I admitted. "I always figured I'd know what to say in the moment."

Devon sighed softly. "I don't," he said.

"I can help you," I said, leaning over the side of the bed. "We'll—"

"Figure it out," he said. "Sure. Night, Kimmy."

"Good night."

It took a while after that for me to settle enough to fall asleep, but I must have eventually because something woke me up.

I lay in my bed, squinting in the dark, trying to figure out what had done it and froze at the sight of two glowing blue eyes staring at me.

Chapter Twelve

A finger poked my cheek.

Flailing, I smacked it away and fumbled to turn on the lamp on the nightstand.

Devon stood leaning over me.

And his eyes were undeniably glowing bright blue.

"Devon?" I whispered.

He didn't say anything, just tilted his head as he stared.

"You're freaking me out," I said, scrambling up from my bed to stand on the other side and put some distance between us.

Devon narrowed his eyes and let out a quiet hum. Then he turned, his movements strangely jerky as he headed for the door.

Oh, no, no, no.

Nearly tripping over my feet, I threw myself between him and his escape route. "Stop." I spread my arms across the wood behind me. "You know you can't leave."

His hand shot out and grabbed the doorknob. I fought to pull his fingers away as he kept trying to twist it. Devon sneered at me as he leaned in close. His mouth opened and closed a few times before he finally managed to speak.

"He's mine," a woman's voice rasped.

I froze at the sound and Devon took the opportunity to lunge for the door handle again.

"I said stop it," I whisper-shouted as I shoved him back. Enough of this. Making a silent promise to apologize to him later, I hooked my leg around Devon's and pushed him down to the floor. The move took him by surprise and he lay there, stunned. I used that to my advantage as I sat on him and reached to snag the sheet off my bed.

"I don't know what's going on, but you are *not* leaving this room." Twisting the sheet around him, I made it as tight as I could before shoving him back so I could tie the ends to the bedpost. Triple-knotted.

He struggled to get free, glaring as the glow in his eyes flickered. "*Mine.*" Devon's head fell forward, eyes closed.

"Hey." I crept closer. "Devon?"

Silence.

I poked his shoulder gently.

He let out a soft snore and I sat back in relief.

A quick internal check showed our connection still holding strong. A few hours ago, I wouldn't have believed I'd be so happy about that.

After a brief debate, I decided to leave him tied up. I shimmied back and sat against the door. The side table lamp was still on, but I didn't have the energy to get up and turn it off. Every muscle in my body was *vibrating*. I wrapped my arms around my knees as I replayed the last few minutes in my mind.

What *was* that? *Who* was that? Why—

Okay. Deep breaths. In. And out. I focused on that for a few minutes until I settled.

He's mine.

That's what the voice said. And whoever it was had been able to *take over* his body so they must have some kind of connection. Question after question ricocheted around in my brain as I watched Devon sleep, but not one single answer. I had no idea what I was dealing with. Or how to deal with it. I dropped my forehead down to rest on my knees.

Grandma. I need you.

✳ ✳ ✳

"Kimmy."

I groaned as I struggled to open my eyes, shifting my back against the hard surface of the door—of the door? Oh, right. I raised a hand to block the light streaming through my bedroom window and spotted Devon shooting me a glare from his spot on the floor.

"Kimmy," he repeated. "*Why* am I tied up?" He struggled against the sheet that was not giving an inch.

"It was for your own good," I said with a yawn, rubbing my eyes. I'd stayed up as long as I could keeping watch and puzzling my way through what we knew so far. I'd cobbled a theory together. A terrifying theory that I was not a fan of, but it was the only thing that made sense.

"Well, can you please untie me?" Devon wiggled restlessly. "I need to go."

"You can't leave." I frowned at him. I thought he understood—

"*No,*" he said through gritted teeth. "I need to *go*. Pee, Kimmy! I need to pee!"

"Oh! Sorry." I scrambled across the floor and untied the sheet. He sprung to his feet as soon as he was free and shot out the door. "Wait!" I dropped my outstretched hand with a groan. I should have checked to make sure my parents weren't around.

Creeping over to my door, I peeked out into the hall. Devon was already in the bathroom with the door closed and the upstairs was quiet, but I could hear the faint clinking of dishes from the kitchen. Mom and Alex were having breakfast. Good. That gave us a bit of space.

By the time Devon came back, I had the sheets and blankets tidied on my bed. He flopped down on top, ruining the effect.

"You going to tell me why I was tied up?" He stared at me with an unimpressed look.

"You don't remember?" I asked and he threw his hands up while shaking his head. "That actually makes sense. You weren't really . . . present."

"Explain? Please?" Devon grumbled as he propped himself up on one elbow.

I sat down beside him and tried to figure out how to explain that he'd basically been possessed. "Last night, I woke up and you were standing over my bed. Your eyes were . . . glowing."

"*Glowing?*"

"Bright blue." I nodded. "You spoke with someone else's voice. She took over your body. Through magic."

His eyes went wide. "Did I try to hurt you?"

"No," I said quickly. "She was trying to make you walk out of the room. That's why I tied you up. I couldn't think of any other way to keep you safe."

"*Oh*. Uh, thank you for that, then, I guess." He moved to sit cross-legged beside me and shook his head. "I don't understand. What did she want with *me*?"

"She said you were *hers*." I got a chill down my spine remembering that voice.

Devon paled. "Do you think she had something to do with how I—how I *died*?" He whispered the last part and I nodded. Awful as it was, it made the most sense.

"I think she took your spark," I said. "And I don't think you're the only one. For months now, everyone coming through the funeral home has been missing a spark. That's *never* happened before. The odd person here and there, but—I thought it was my fault."

Months of being mad at myself for not knowing how to use the power on my own. Months of thinking it was *their* fault. Being mad at them for not having any unfinished business. Being mad at Grandma—

I felt sick at the idea that this person could have taken all of their sparks.

Taken Grandma's.

"But you brought it back," Devon said. "My spark. That's why I'm alive again, right? Is that why she came after me?"

"I'm still not sure how I managed to do that," I admitted. "But I think that's why she tried to make you leave." She must need him around to take the spark back. "The important thing right now is to keep you hidden while we work on getting to the bottom of it all." Keeping an eye on Devon was the only way I could protect him at the moment.

"I was thinking I should go home?" he asked, gnawing at his lip.

"No!" How could he even suggest that? "This person must be a powerful witch. She's stolen the lives of who knows how many people. She has to be responsible for that huge memory spell as well. And she's looking for you. Most likely to steal your spark again!"

"Yeah, but we don't know how far the memory spell goes, do we? What if my *parents* are looking for me?" He started to climb off the bed. "They'll be worried."

"You could lead the witch right to them," I said, pulling him back. "Do you want to put them in danger?"

Devon had a silent battle with himself before shaking his head.

"I know this is scary," I said. "But I'm—"

"Stop telling me you're going to figure this out! Please." He cut me off with a sharp wave of his hand. "You might be a kid with magic, but you're still a *kid*. What can you actually do?"

"Apparently I'm capable of a lot more than I thought I was, so who knows?" We hadn't even made our way through all of the journals yet. There had to be something helpful there.

Pushing forward was how I'd brought back Devon. If I kept pushing forward on this, the answers had to come together eventually. *Try, try again.*

"Do you think you can trust me for a little bit longer?" I asked Devon.

He scrubbed his hands over his face and groaned. "Fine."

"Great," I said, hustling out of bed. "Are you hungry?"

"I could eat."

"I'll be right back. Stay here and—"

"Be quiet," he finished, flopping backward onto the covers. "I know."

Morris was waiting outside my door when I opened it so I let him in to keep Devon company while I was gone. I zipped down to the kitchen, hoping for a quick in and out.

"Morning!" Alex greeted me as I made a beeline for the

toaster. He and Mom were seated at the table, empty plates in front of them and nearly empty coffee mugs in hand.

"We had two new guests arrive this morning," Mom said to me. "I'll be working on them this afternoon if you decide you'd like to try to Wake them before that."

"I can't believe old Mr. Kingsley passed," Alex said, shaking his head. "We ran into each other at the farmers market this weekend and he was the picture of good health."

I paused in my toast making. "Do you know how he died?"

"The most peaceful way you can," Mom said. "In his sleep. So did Mrs. Manning, come to think of it. Both of them, late last night. Different retirement homes, though."

Tug, tug, tug.

I didn't need a warning from my power to be suspicious of these new arrivals. They fit the profile of every single individual with no remaining spark who'd come through the funeral home over the past few months.

They could be the witch's latest victims. My stomach turned slowly at the thought.

There was a whirlwind of activity as Mom and Alex finished off their coffees and dealt with the dishes. "Let me know if you want to go downstairs," Mom said, giving me a hug before heading to her office.

Alex ruffled my hair with a smile. "No visitations today," he said. "How about a family game night?"

"Sure," I said. "Sounds great." The threat of an increasing body count was motivation enough to solve this quickly, but the promise of UNO didn't hurt.

After whipping up four pieces of toast and peanut butter at lightning speed, I returned to my room. Devon hadn't moved from his spot and was now gently petting Morris, who was purring up a storm.

"Breakfast is served," I said as I shut the door behind me.

He eyed the plates in my hands with interest. "Peanut butter toast? Gimme."

I passed one over and moved to sit beside him. We ate in silence for a bit, but it wasn't too long before Devon started shooting me curious looks.

"Wha' g'in on?" he finally asked, talking around the wad of toast in his mouth.

For a second I was convinced Grandma Bev herself reached through the beyond to speak through my mouth when I replied, "Chew, swallow, and *then* talk, please."

Devon chewed obnoxiously, swallowed, and then opened his mouth wide to show it was empty. "What's going on?" he repeated. "You're all frowny."

Time to bring him up to speed.

"Two new people were brought in this morning," I said, setting my plate aside, appetite gone. "I think they might also be victims of this witch. If my theory is correct."

"How do we test your theory?" he asked, taking another huge bite.

"We take a little field trip to the basement," I said.

Chapter Thirteen

When Devon stopped short at the bottom of the stairs, I realized I could have done a better job *preparing* him for the prep room. I forgot people weren't used to it like I was.

His eyes caught on the sheet-covered tables in the middle of the room. "Are those? Um? You know . . ."

"Guests is what Mom likes to call them," I said as I sidled around him and made my way into the room. "You're okay to come in. Just be respectful."

"Respectful." He nodded, looking a little green. "I can do that. Hello." Devon waved at the tables, still keeping his distance. "It's okay that they're sitting out like that?"

"The embalming process works best with a warmer body so—"

"Nope, I already regret asking." Devon turned away, shaking his head. "Gimme a minute." He took a few slow breaths before finally noticing the rest of the room. "Wait, is that an elevator?" He pointed at the far wall with a confused squawk. "Why is there an elevator?"

"For bringing gurneys down when people arrive and for taking caskets up to the viewing room. Do *not* get in there," I said, waving a firm finger at him, ignoring the scrunched nose I got in return. "Stay clear and keep your hands to yourself."

"What are you going to do?" Curiosity won out and Devon came over to join me, arms crossed as he leaned in. "How are you testing the theory?"

"I'm going to try to Wake them," I said. It was risky, but it was the only thing I could think of. The only thing I *knew*.

"Wait, what?" Devon shot a look at the tables and then back at me. "Why? What if—what if they *are* like me and they stay awake? What are you going to do with three not-dead people walking around? Won't that make us a bigger target for the witch?"

"I don't know! I'll fig—"

"You need to stop saying that," Devon snapped.

"Listen," I said. "If the witch *didn't* kill them, there's

two other possible outcomes." I ticked them off on my fingers. "One, they have a remaining spark and it'll be a normal Waking. Two, they truly won't have any unfinished business and they won't Wake at all."

"But you don't think it's going to be either of those," he pointed out. "You think it was the witch."

"Yeah, and that's all the more reason to do this." I held out a hand to try to halt the argument ready to burst out of him. "When we help people with unfinished business, their spark is at peace when I let it go," I said. "If there's a chance that these two have been snatched away by an evil witch, I don't want to *leave* them with her. Not when they deserve to rest."

Like Grandma should be.

If I'd pushed through with her, if Mom hadn't *stopped* me, we'd have known—

I shook off those thoughts. There wasn't time to dwell on that right now. I couldn't do anything about Grandma. It had been months since she died and there was no body to pull her back to since she'd been cremated.

But I *could* try to do something for these two. Who knew what was happening to them right now? Keeping them here with us had to be the better option even if things got . . . complicated.

"Okay." Devon sighed. "Be careful, I guess?" He stepped aside so I could get to work. No sooner had my fingers touched the sheet covering Mr. Kingsley when I heard someone opening the door at the top of the stairs. I whirled around.

"Go, go, go!" Shoving Devon ahead of me, I made a beeline for the cleaning supplies closet. We barely managed to get inside before whoever was on the stairs arrived in the prep room for what better be some incredibly pressing business. I cracked open the door the tiniest bit to try to see who it was.

"Oof!" I pushed back at Devon as he tried to peek, too. After a brief elbow war, we both managed to find spots to spy from. Soon enough the intruder came into view.

Tamsin.

She had a leather bag with her that she slung onto the tray table as she hummed to herself. Rolling the tray closer to the tables, she stopped and put her hands on her hips. "Let's see what's going on here with you," she said.

"Kimmy," Devon whispered urgently in my ear. "Is she going to start doing funeral home stuff right now because I don't want to watch that."

"No," I said, shushing him. At least, she shouldn't be,

considering Tamsin wasn't qualified for that. What exactly *was* she up to?

Carefully pulling the sheet back from Mr. Kingsley, Tamsin looked him over, mumbling to herself. She reached into the bag she'd set on the tray table and pulled out . . . a rock?

A sparkly black rock.

She held her hand out palm up over Mr. Kingsley and laid the rock in the center of it. The mumbling started up again. Then the rock began to glow and so did her *tattoos*.

"Kimmy," Devon whispered.

"Yeah, I see it." I could hardly believe it, but I saw it. And I had no idea what it meant.

"Do you think she's the one behind this? The one who—"

"I don't know! Stop talking," I muttered. I wanted to dismiss the idea entirely. Tamsin was friendly and kind, but I had to look at all the facts.

She'd shown up not too long after the no-spark people started coming in to the funeral home. She clearly had magic. She was acting off yesterday, *and* why had she been at the hospital? The picture I was starting to put together didn't look good. The voice that came out of Devon hadn't sounded like hers, but could they be working together?

"What's she doing now? Shouldn't we stop her?" Devon straightened up and I pulled him close before he dove out into the room.

"We don't know what she's doing," I whispered, holding his arm tight. "We have to be careful. If she's involved, that means she—"

"Killed me," Devon whispered.

The door swung open and Tamsin appeared, glowering down at us.

"Ahhhh!" We both screamed, falling to the floor.

"Don't kill me again!" Devon cried.

"Whoa! Whoa." Tamsin stepped back with her hands in the air. "*What* are you talking about?" She darted a glance over at me. "What's going on?"

"Nothing!" I hauled Devon up to his feet with me and we inched our way out of the closet. "He's joking. We were playing a game."

I weighed our options as my heart pounded in my chest. Tamsin was between us and the stairs so that was a no-go, and she could easily catch us if we went for the elevator.

If she was as strong as the evil witch, she probably wouldn't even have to move to do it.

One wrong step and she could take us out.

Except . . .

Why hadn't she done anything yet?

She stood there with her arms up and her eyes wide, staring at the two of us. No. Staring at Devon. *"Your aura,"* she gasped.

"What's happening?" Devon murmured to me. "Why aren't we escaping?"

That snapped Tamsin out of it. "We need to talk," she said, stepping forward with her hands outstretched, which had us cringing back.

"Talk is code for murder," Devon whispered in my ear and I shrugged him off.

"Kimmy, this may come as a shock," Tamsin said, focusing her attention on me. "And believe me, I know how it sounds, but . . . you have magic." She paused, clearly giving me a moment, which was nice, because *what?*

"Yes," I said slowly. "I know, but—"

"You *know?* Thank goodness." Tamsin sagged as she let out a relieved sigh. "I wasn't sure if your grandma had a chance to tell you anything or if you were totally in the dark and I've been so stressed about how to bring it up and then *yesterday*, your aura was basically exploding and I was worried you were accessing power without knowing how to handle it—"

"Tamsin." I tried to wade in on her rambling.

"And now here you are with a resurrected kid," she said, pointing at Devon who was still trying to edge farther away, tugging me along with him. "Which we definitely need to talk about, but it'll be *so* much easier if you already know about magic—"

"Tamsin! Stop for one second," I yelled, cutting her off abruptly so I could think. I let her words settle between us. I really hoped I wasn't mistaken, but something was telling me Tamsin was on our side. "I think she's okay," I said to Devon.

"Oh, good." He instantly relaxed. "I was not prepared to fight an evil witch's accomplice."

"Evil wi—" Tamsin lurched forward, laser focused. "You've seen her?"

"No," I stammered out. "I only heard her voice—"

She turned away abruptly, moving to cover Mr. Kingsley again. Then she grabbed one of the stools and sat down. "I need you to tell me everything."

"You want us to spill our guts without you telling *us* anything?" I was tired of flailing around trying to put things together. "How do *you* know about magic? How do you know about the witch?"

"I tracked her here," Tamsin said. "It's kind of a long story that I *promise* I will tell you, but she's a very dangerous individual, Kimmy. If I'm going to be able to help, I need to have the full picture, so please give me a bit of trust and tell me what happened."

She rested her elbows on her knees, steepling her fingers under her chin. Ready for me to share all of my secrets, which was something that didn't come naturally to me as a Jones.

How could I know if she was fully trustworthy?

Tug, tug, tug.

That helped me relax. The tugs in my chest had led me to helping Devon and discovering what the witch was up to so hopefully they weren't steering me wrong here, either.

Also, I had a tiny flicker of . . . excitement? Tamsin was the first magic user I'd ever met outside of Grandma. I wanted to jump inside her brain, dig around, and soak up everything she knew. Including, hopefully, how to deal with an evil, life-force-stealing witch.

"I'll start at the beginning," I said, pulling my own stool over while Devon made himself comfortable on the computer chair. I told her all about the dozens of people who'd come through with no remaining spark, including Grandma. Then being woken up yesterday morning by the tugs and hearing the news about Devon, which led to my break-in at the morgue.

"The news." Tamsin frowned. "I didn't hear any—ah. Memory spell. Clever. That must have been why I was at the hospital."

"I saw you," I exclaimed. "At first, I thought Mom had sent you after me."

"No, if I heard that story, I would have wanted to investigate," she said, shaking her head. "I found myself in the elevator with no idea what I was there for."

"Do you know a lot about memory spells?" Devon asked, rolling his chair closer to our huddle. "Like have people only forgotten what happened or—"

"Depends on what her goal was," Tamsin said hesitantly. "But it could be a complete erasure." As in, no one would remember Devon at all.

He slowly slumped back in his seat, face pale as he took that in.

"Maybe it's not," I said quietly, trying to catch his eye. "And if it is, we'll—"

"Yeah, I know," he said, cutting me off with a wave. "Just finish telling her the story."

"Okay, uh, once I got into the morgue, I tried to Wake Devon," I said, and explained everything that followed from managing to Wake him, sneaking him home, finding out about the memory wipe, having the witch possess him, realizing she was stealing life forces, and ending here in the prep room with Tamsin.

Our new employee who *also* had magic. Guess she didn't put that on her résumé.

"Wow," Tamsin said, rubbing a hand over her forehead. "So you—and then—oh, she must have used the storm to power the memory spell, smart, and—okay, this explains so much."

To *her*. "Now it's your turn." I scooted my stool closer and Devon followed with a flurry of wheel squeaks. "What do you know about the witch? Why were you tracking her? What kind of powers do *you* have? How did you know about our family? Did you know my grandma? Is that why you came to work here? What did you mean about my aura?"

"Also, what's an aura?" Devon added, raising his hand in question.

I turned to him. "You don't know?"

"Do *you*?"

"Of course, I do," I scoffed. "It's a—it's like a—"

Hunh.

"It's an energy field around your body," Tamsin explained. "People like me who can see them are able to gather information about your state of being."

"You can do that?" Devon exclaimed. "What's mine like?"

"Yours is dimmed and, well, fractured." Tamsin winced. "Which makes sense since you only have a portion of your life force and there are remnants of the witch's magic influencing it as well as Kimmy's."

"I was hoping for something cool." Devon sighed. "Like Kimmy's exploding one."

"Is that cool, though?" I asked Tamsin. "Aren't explosions usually bad?"

Tamsin's eyes went unfocused as she looked more around me than at me. She traced a hand through the air above my head. "It's four times the size of what it was and *so* much brighter. If you've been using your power all along, why would—"

Tamsin gasped. "That's how you were able to steal Devon back!" she said, her voice turning faintly accusing. "You broke the cap! *How*?"

"What about this whole conversation makes you think I'd know the answer to that?" I had no idea why it worked. Why I'd been able to break it when Dad couldn't. Why was she asking me when she clearly knew more about magic and . . . hang on. "How do *you* know about the cap on our magic?"

"How do I—*oh*." Tamsin's face did a complicated dance as she looked everywhere but at me. "I guess we are going to have that awkward magic discussion after all."

"Tamsin!" I snapped. People giving me bits of information as they saw fit was getting me *nowhere*.

Her next words came out in a rush. "I know because my family put it there."

Chapter Fourteen

"Y*ou* put the cap on our magic?"

"Not me specifically," Tamsin said. "Someone way back in my family tree—"

"Can you tell me why?" I leaned forward, excitement bubbling up. "Grandma never did and I haven't found anything in our family journals yet. I don't know what was so dangerous about our power that they would do that."

Devon waved a hand in the air. "I mean, bringing people back to life?" He gestured to himself and shrugged. "I can see how that would spiral. Crowd control, for one."

I couldn't argue with that, but still—

"Was that the only reason?" I asked Tamsin. "Or was there something else?"

A complicated look crossed her face, there and gone in an instant, but I jumped on it. "What? What do you know?"

"I don't *know* anything, but I might have a way to find out." She reached over and rummaged through her bag, pulling out a tablet. "The Bly family records."

"Everything's on there?"

"Yup," Tamsin said proudly. "Well, I can access them through it. My older sisters and I have spent years digitizing everything and creating a searchable database."

"Wow." I loved our Jones family journals, but a *searchable database*? That would have made my life easier lately. "If we type in my family name, all your records on us will pop up?"

"Yes?" Tamsin cringed. "But accessing it will depend on whether or not either of you are any good at hacking passwords."

"Did you lock yourself out?" Devon laughed.

"No, my parents did." She looked down at the tablet with a scowl. "I didn't think they knew how to do that," she muttered.

"Why would they lock you out?"

"I—" Tamsin began. "The thing is—technically—I'm not supposed to be tracking the witch right now."

She looked so guilty, I was almost afraid to ask. "Where are you supposed to be?"

"College?" Tamsin twisted her hands around the tablet. "They wanted me to stop thinking about the family business and focus on school."

"That's going well," Devon said, stretching out an arm to make grabby hands at the tablet. Tamsin opened it to the database before handing it over.

"I'm on it." Devon grinned at her, settling back in his chair as he started to spin it in a lazy circle. "Which old person password should we try first? Zero, zero, zero, zero? Or maybe one, two, three, four. Hmm."

At least he'd be occupied for a while. I turned to Tamsin. "How did you know about me if you can't get into your records?"

"I'd looked up your family just before I got locked out," she said. "I knew we'd helped with a power cap and house protection, but that's it." Tamsin shifted uncomfortably in her seat. "I was going to contact your grandma, but . . ."

Grandma had already died by then.

"I thought staying close wouldn't be a bad idea since I wasn't sure what you knew or how you were handling things," she said. "I was sticking around to track the witch anyway so it was kind of a two birds, one stone thing."

"Hey, why hasn't your family capped the witch?" Devon asked, peering at us over the top of the tablet as he slouched in the chair, feet slung over the side. "Boom. Problem solved."

"Oh, we've tried," Tamsin said, shoving her rock back into her bag somewhat aggressively. "When a magic user spirals out of control, our family is part of the group that gets called on by the community to help. It's been our mission to stop her for more than a hundred years."

"A hundred years of stealing other people's lives." I couldn't believe it.

Devon tilted his head to look at Tamsin. "Why does she do it? Does anyone know?"

"*That* I have studied," she said. "She's had many names, but she was born Cecilia West and her magic was originally based in healing. Normally, people with that type of power pull energy from nature, but every source has a finite amount. You can only gather so much strength from a plant or a crystal."

Tamsin sighed. "Her entire family contracted tuberculosis. She was the only one with magic, and she wasn't able to save them," she said. "When *she* fell ill, she was all alone. Her power twisted in an effort to save herself and pulled energy from people throughout her town instead. She stole enough life forces to heal and disappeared."

"But she came back," I said, dreading where this was going.

"Twisting her power like that corrupted it," Tamsin said. "It continuously needs a larger amount to sustain it. Over the years, the length of her disappearances keeps decreasing and her hunting period is increasing."

"Would you call that a *catch*?" Devon asked and I stuck a foot out to tap his chair, slowly spinning him around to face the other way.

"The catch or the cost, sure," Tamsin said. "My family got involved after she returned the first time and left a trail of bodies. They tracked her down and tried to set a cap, but she blew right through it and disappeared again. Most magic users can't do that."

She sent a pointed look at me.

"But Cecilia had the benefit from the power of extra life forces on her side," Tamsin continued. "She got another boost when she pulled them from the people who tried to stop her."

Killing Tamsin's ancestors.

"She's powerful," Tamsin said. "And even though she needs more and more to maintain that power, she'll never stop because it's the only thing keeping her alive."

Leaning back, Tamsin rubbed at her eyes. "She's smart

and keeps adapting," she said. "Every time she comes back, she's got a new trick. The third time around, she'd learned how to bind her energy to another person so she could take over a new body. That's made it harder to track her through non-magical ways."

So, we didn't even know what she looked like. Great.

"Plus, she's learned other forms of magic, like the memory spell," Tamsin said.

"Wouldn't stuff like that use up more of her power?" I asked.

"From what you told me, I think she took advantage of the storm to power it," Tamsin said. "Thinking on her feet is another reason she's survived this long."

Tamsin made her sound indestructible. "Are you saying there's nothing we can do to stop her? We let her keep killing until she's had her fill and disappears again?"

"No," Tamsin said firmly. "That's why I'm here. To stop her. Once and for all."

Chapter Fifteen

"**W**hat are *you* going to do about an evil witch that *no one* has been able to stop in one hundred years?" I threw my hands up.

"Ugh, you sound like my parents." Tamsin groaned.

"It's not my birthday," Devon declared. He looked up at our silence and noticed our stares. "For the database. The password. Not my—uh, sorry, what did I miss?"

"Tamsin's going to stop the witch," I said and he perked up in his seat.

"Cool," he said. "How?"

"Yeah, Tamsin. *How?*" After the story she'd told, it sounded pretty freaking impossible.

"I created a *new* spell," she said, a huge grin splitting her face.

"You can do that?" Grandma had only ever taught me how to use *our* magic. I had no idea you could do other things. Or maybe we couldn't. Maybe it was only Tamsin and her family.

I hated this. There were *so many* things I still didn't know.

"Absolutely, but this is even cooler than you think." Tamsin bounced up from her seat and pointed at the tablet in Devon's hands. "It's like how we brought the records up to date, but I'm doing that with magic. I'm mixing it with modern technology."

"The spell is in the tablet?" Devon scrunched his face at the look she gave him. "What? It would not be the weirdest thing I've come across lately, okay?"

"It's a real live spell," Tamsin said. "I used trace evidence found on some of the victims to zero in on the biometric and magical markers of the witch. Her personal magical signature. I crafted a spell that will target her *specifically*." She held out her arms, pausing for effect. "It will eliminate her magic."

"Whoa," I said. "That sounds effective." Tamsin nodded enthusiastically.

"Why isn't your family here helping you catch her?"

Devon piped up. "Isn't this the spell you've all been waiting for?"

"Well." Tamsin cleared her throat. "I haven't been able to actually test it yet."

I side-eyed Devon, who was looking like he shared my concerns with that revelation.

"I *can't* test it because it's designed specifically for the witch," she explained in a rush. "I could craft one for someone else to see if the spell works, but . . ."

"Then that person would lose their magic," I finished for her.

"Exactly." She sighed.

"I can see why your family might not want to take a chance on an untested spell," I said carefully.

Tamsin scrubbed a hand through her curls as she strode around the room. "But I've made all kinds of other spells and potions and things that *have* worked. I'm twenty years old! I've been working in the family business for years. I wish they'd have a little more faith in me."

"Maybe it's not a lack of faith and more that they don't want you to die," Devon said, shrugging when she heaved out a sigh at him. "Just a thought."

"I know." Tamsin nodded, falling back onto her stool. "That's why I was doing this on my own. *I'm* willing to risk my life for the chance at stopping her from hurting anyone else. That's my choice to make."

"Aren't you worried about someone from your family showing up?" I asked her. "They're still hunting her, right?"

"Half of them are working on trying to strengthen the same old spells that they keep using, and the others?" Tamsin flushed and looked down at her shoes. "I may have sent some fake tips from a few different burner accounts to put them on a false trail. I think my cousins are searching in Vancouver at the moment?"

"Nice," Devon said and I swatted at him.

"Listen," Tamsin said. "I needed to give myself time to work because I *know* I can do this. All I have to do is identify the witch, trap her, and then my spell will take care of the rest!"

"Destroy a witch in these three easy steps," Devon chirped.

I groaned. "*How* do we identify her? Where should we start?"

"I've been tracking her pattern of behavior," Tamsin said, pulling her phone out of her bag. She unlocked it and opened her notes app. "Staying in one place for so long is unusual for her, but if your grandma was actually her first victim, it makes sense. It would have given her a boost and she might be hoping there are other magic users in town for her to drain."

I didn't want to think too much about her targeting me or Tamsin. "Everyone after Grandma has been elderly people from long-term care homes. Where does Devon fit?"

"Taking the life force of a regular adult is a meal. A magic user is a feast. But a kid?" Tamsin turned to Devon thoughtfully. "You said you were out watching the meteor shower when she found you?"

He nodded, straightening up in his chair.

"Ah. A young life force combined with the power of a celestial event would've been a big boost for her, too," she said. "I think Devon was a crime of opportunity."

The dots started connecting. "The park is close to Basbridge Retirement Village," I said. "I bet she came across him after stealing the life from someone else over there."

"If that's her hunting grounds, maybe that's the area where I need to set my trap," Tamsin mused, making more notes in her phone. "Another piece of the plan comes together."

Now that I had all of this new information swirling around in my brain, I was realizing we might be the next piece her plan was missing.

Tug, tug, tug.

Yeah, I was on to something here. "You said she's always been too strong because of the extra life forces, right?"

Tamsin nodded, waiting for me to continue.

I pointed at Devon. "I stole his spark back, but I'm not sure if I got it all because it looked weird—"

"Hey," Devon complained half-heartedly.

"*Would* that have had an effect?" I asked Tamsin.

"Yes," she said, considering the possibility. "But I'm not sure how much—"

"What if I took two more?" I walked over to the tables holding Mr. Kingsley and Mrs. Manning.

"That might make a difference. Maybe all the difference." Tamsin's eyes went wide before turning calculated. "But can you do that? Having full access to your power is one thing, but there's no guarantee you could maintain a hold on three sparks or what kind of strain it would cause," she muttered, staring at me like I was a particularly annoying math problem. "Would it be better to—what am I doing?"

Tamsin gave her head a fierce shake. "It's one thing to take calculated risks for myself, but I can't involve the two of you."

"It's a little late for that," I said and Devon raised his hand.

"For the record," he said. "I'm already more involved than I'd like to be."

I ignored him and focused on Tamsin. "You're sure your spell could work," I said. "I'm sure my magic will hold."

Tug, tug, tug.

Tamsin sighed. "We don't even know if these two are her victims or not," she said. "I was interrupted by people whisper-yelling in the closet before I could finish checking."

"We have to find out before Mom comes down to prep them," I said. "It's better if they haven't been—"

"Please don't finish that sentence," Devon said, voice weary. "I'm maxed out on things I've learned against my will this week."

"I can finish checking," Tamsin said, retrieving her bag and digging out the black rock. "Then we'll know for sure and can go from there." She went over to pull back the sheet on Mr. Kingsley. As she held out her hand over his body, the rock started to glow gently.

I knew exactly what it was going to prove.

The witch had taken them.

Tug, tug, tug.

They were going to be *stuck* there without any way out.

Stuck when I *knew* I could help.

I could bring them back.

Tug, tug, TUG.

"Uh, Kimmy?" Devon whispered.

"What," I snapped, looking down when he pointed at my hands. Which were glowing.

"I'm finding traces of her magic here," Tamsin said, freezing when she caught sight of my hands. "What is that?"

"My power." I brought my hands up to stare at them. "It did this when I Woke Devon, but I don't—I don't understand. I'm not—"

I was going to say not trying to use it, but all of a sudden, I realized I *was* using it. It surged through me along with a need to *do* something—to search, to connect, to bring back what had been stolen.

The light from my hands arced through the air and into Mr. Kingsley and Mrs. Manning. Forging the connection on its own. "How is it—it can't do that unless I'm touching them," I whispered.

"Pull it back, Kimmy," Tamsin said firmly. She stepped beside me and tried to touch my shoulder, wincing when she got too close. "Focus. You can do it."

She didn't understand. I couldn't. I wasn't in control. This was all the power.

How was I supposed to stop it?

It flooded through the two bodies, searching for what they'd lost. Pushing forward and dragging me along with it. A wave of dizziness crashed over me, but the power didn't let me fall.

TUG, TUG, TUG.

In the distant corner of my mind, I found them. Two bundles of energy that were bright, but torn and cold. Tumultuous. Just like Devon's had been. The power grabbed them and *pulled*. It yanked them free and wrapped energy around them until they were warm and settled and anchored into place.

Finally, it relented, flowing back and settling into my chest where it belonged. I relaxed for one moment and then everything went dark.

Chapter Sixteen

I opened my eyes and blinked against the brightness of the fluorescent lights.

Grandma was right. They were unpleasant.

"Hey." Devon's face came into view. "You're awake."

"Kind of." I groaned. It was loud. There was yelling. So much yelling. My head was pounding. "What happened?"

"Your power went all '*raawr*,'" he said, making claw hands in the air. "And then you fell over. I thought you were dead for a second, but then I saw you were still breathing." He side-eyed me. "Did you bring yourself back? Are we not-*dead* dead twins now?"

"Please stop talking," I said as I tried to sit up. Devon gave me a hand and we managed to get me on my feet.

The source of the yelling then became clear.

"Oh, yeah," Devon said. "And you brought that guy back, too."

"What kind of people play a sick joke like this on an old man!" Mr. Kingsley was sitting on the table, his legs dangling over the side as he fought to straighten out his sweater.

"Please, Mr. Kingsley," Tamsin said, hands clasped in front of her chest. "If you would let me explain—"

"Nope. Don't bother." He wagged a finger at her. "I used to be an insurance investigator. I can tell when somebody's about to tell me a pack of lies. What I *want*—"

"So much yelling," I whimpered. His voice was like a continuous spike through my skull.

"Kimmy!" Tamsin gasped. "You're awake. Are you hurt?"

"—is for someone to help me down from this infernal thing!" Mr. Kingsley wiggled as he tried to slide his way off the table while patting at his pockets with one hand. *"And where are my dang glasses?"*

The door to the basement opened and shut quickly, followed by the sound of footsteps rushing down the stairs. "What on earth is going on down here—"

Alex halted on the last step, eyes going wide as he

took in the sight before him. "Kimmy," he said, his voice sounding a bit strangled. "How, um . . . *alive* . . . why . . ." He rubbed a hand over his chin when words failed him.

As he opened his mouth to try again, there was a rustling noise as the sheet on the second table began to move.

"Hello?" a muffled voice called.

Tamsin and I met each other's horrified eyes. *Mrs. Manning.*

"You brought her back, too?" Tamsin cried. "Kimmy!"

"Not on purpose!" I held my head as another bout of dizziness hit. Devon stepped closer, hands hovering like he was ready to catch me and I waved him off.

"Is anyone there?" Mrs. Manning called.

Lunging around Mr. Kingsley to the other table, Tamsin gently peeled back the sheet.

Mrs. Manning peered up at her. "Have I been kidnapped?"

"No, ma'am," Tamsin said. "You're at the funeral home."

"Oh, that's too bad. Waking up under that sheet in a strange room, I thought for sure I'd been kidnapped," she mused. "It would have been excellent material for my book."

"Sorry to disappoint you?" Tamsin said, more than a bit bewildered as she helped her to sit up.

Alex caught my eye from across the room. *"What did you do?"* he mouthed at me.

"I don't know!" I mouthed back.

"Her book? Is she joking?" Mr. Kingsley huffed. "This is—I woke up in a *morgue*. I want some answers! And my glasses!"

"Cabinet," Alex murmured to Tamsin.

"Right." She snapped her fingers as she headed over to the cabinet where we kept people's personal items like jewelry and glasses until they were finished being prepped. She located them quickly and Mr. Kingsley snatched them out of her hand with a grunt.

"That's a start."

"I know this is confusing." I stepped forward, finally steady enough to do so. "But I'm going to try to give you as many answers as I can." Aiming for gentle but straightforward, I broke the news of their deaths and my magic bringing them back and let that sink in.

Better to give them a moment before I brought the evil witch into the mix.

"Magic," Mr. Kingsley scoffed. "Are you buying this?" He turned to Mrs. Manning, scowling when she nodded sagely.

"My grandmother had magic," she said. "Hedge witch. Her gardens were a thing of beauty. I didn't inherit her power, but still—always neat to have a witch in the family tree."

Mr. Kingsley snorted. "Prove it," he said, crossing his arms as he glared at the whole room. "Prove this magic exists."

"Well, if I demonstrate mine, you'll go back to rest and nobody would be proving anything to you because you'd be dead," I said.

That was a bold-faced lie since I could tell the connections with him and Mrs. Manning were as locked as Devon's. They weren't going anywhere at the moment.

But his tone was making me cranky so he didn't need to know that.

Yet.

"Are you *threatening* me—"

"I have something," Tamsin declared, reaching down to grab her bag off the floor. She pulled out a pink crystal. "This is rose quartz," she said as she stepped over to Mr. Kingsley.

"If you think some *rock* is going to convince me—what is that? What are you doing?"

The crystal in Tamsin's hand had begun to glow as

she held it close to his chest. "It helps relieve stress and anxiety," she said as one of the intricate tattoos on her arm also started to pulse with a soft light. "A little cleanse."

"This is ridiculous." His heavy eyebrows bunched together. "I don't see how—you can't—wha—" Mr. Kingsley's shoulders relaxed and the tiniest smile quirked at the corner of his mouth. "That's not so bad."

"I have a suspicion that's high praise," Mrs. Manning whispered to Tamsin. "Tell me, what do the tattoos do, dear? They're lovely."

"Thank you." Tamsin blushed. "I designed them myself to help channel energy and—"

"Okay." Alex came forward and clapped his hands once, pulling everyone's attention. "Clearly, we have a lot to talk through and I think we could do it in more comfortable surroundings. Why don't we head up to the kitchen?" He gestured toward the stairs.

Nobody moved. I didn't know about anyone else, but I was too stunned to manage any kind of upward movement.

"There will be snacks," he tried. "And tea?"

"Ooh, I'd love a cup of tea," Mrs. Manning said as she gracefully slid off of her table.

Mr. Kingsley patted his belly. "I could eat," he said before squinting at me. "Hey, wait a minute. We're not going to start craving brains or anything, are we?"

"You're not zombies," I exclaimed.

"She gets sensitive about that," Devon whispered and I elbowed him.

"I think I spotted some cookies earlier," Tamsin said, grabbing her bag and her tablet before herding Mr. Kingsley toward the stairs with Mrs. Manning bringing up the rear.

"Right behind you," Alex called after them before whipping back to face me and throwing his arms out in the air in one gigantic *what?* motion.

"Is it okay for them to go up there?" I whispered. "What if someone sees them?"

He lowered his arms with a sigh. "We have no appointments scheduled and the only other person here is your mom," he said. "She's in the office at the moment. However, after I put the kettle on, I will be bringing her to the kitchen *immediately*."

He shot me a look when I bit back a sigh.

"Don't even try to hide out down here," he said as he also headed upstairs. "Full story. From you. Kitchen. Two minutes."

I took a moment to tidy up before following. Grandma would have thrown a fit if I ever left a mess like this.

"Hey, you okay?" Devon popped up at my side as I

folded one of the sheets, making me flail a bit. I hadn't noticed he'd stayed behind.

"I'm fine," I said. "Just preparing myself for an epic lecture."

"Parents." He nodded. "Speaking of, when do you think we can go check on mine? You said—"

"I know. I'm sorry." There were way too many things piling up at once. "Let's get through this chat and then hopefully we can check on the whole memory thing."

"The whole memory thing," Devon repeated flatly. "Yeah. That would be great."

"I'm serious. I promised you we'd figure it out, and we will." I patted his back and steered him ahead of me. "Come on, we should go before Alex sends my mom down."

"Or Mr. Kingsley eats all the cookies," he added.

Tamsin grabbed me as soon as we entered the kitchen and pulled me off to the side. "Hey," she whispered. "Are you okay? *Don't* lie."

"I'm a little wobbly," I admitted. "Kind of tired. I don't know what happened."

"Your power surged," she said. "It was totally out of your control. That's extremely dangerous, Kimmy. We need to—"

"*What?*"

Whatever she was going to say got cut off by the shriek carrying down the hallway from the office. Rapid steps thumped toward us until Mom appeared in the doorway with Alex close behind. A shaky hand reached up to brace against the frame. Her gaze darted around as she recognized two of our guests as former residents of the prep room.

"Kimmy?" she asked, her voice high and pinched. I could hear all of the unspoken questions in that one word.

What's going on?

Why are the dead people alive?

Who is that boy?

What did you do?

"I can explain," I said immediately. Half of it, at least.

A high shrill scream filled the room.

Oh, right, the kettle.

"Why don't you all have a seat," Alex said as he took it off the burner. "Tea will be ready in a moment and we can talk."

He started sorting out cups while I grabbed the container with the last of the cookies I'd made earlier in the week. Chairs squeaked and scraped as everyone else settled themselves at the table.

Well, not everyone.

"Kimberly Anne Jones." Mom full-named me as she

swept past to open the fridge and dig through the shelves. "I have no words. I cannot believe—how did you even—" She straightened up abruptly with a large plastic container in her hand. "Can they eat watermelon?"

"Yes." I sighed. "Everyone can eat regular food." Honestly.

"Does everyone like watermelon?" she asked the group and was met with a chorus of *yes*es. Muttering about vitamin replenishment, she closed the fridge and brought the container over to the table where Alex was handing out mugs. I followed with the cookies.

With a bit of adjusting, we all managed to fit around the kitchen table. Mom and Alex on one side. Mrs. Manning and Mr. Kingsley on each end. Me, Tamsin, and Devon all stuffed together on the other side, faced with the expectant stares of the others.

"Mom and Alex, you already know some of this, but I think it'll be easier if I start right at the beginning," I said. It was the only way I was going to be able to keep everything straight.

Mrs. Manning and Mr. Kingsley knew the basics of our family power from the chat downstairs, but I went over it again to make sure they understood.

Then I told them about Grandma passing away. All

the people coming through with no remaining sparks and how I was beginning to doubt my power. I told them about everything that had happened with Devon and the morgue. As he chimed in with his own colorful details, I spotted Mom's face growing more and more pinched as she put together the pieces of everything that wasn't said.

"Wait a minute," she said, holding up a hand. "Did you—are you telling me that you *broke the cap?*"

I nodded silently.

"What cap?" Mrs. Manning asked.

Tamsin started explaining to her in a whisper as I watched Mom. Her hands gripped the edge of the table as she stared at me like I was another stranger in her house.

"How?" she finally said. "Are you okay? What does this mean?"

"I don't know how, but I *am* okay," I said, ignoring Tamsin's look. "As for what it means? I think there's more to the story that you should hear first."

I told them about the witch and everything that had happened because of her. How there were now connections that couldn't be broken.

Tamsin filled them in on what she knew about the witch's history and how her own family factored into it all, plus the spell she'd created that she hoped would defeat the witch.

If we were lucky.

"Wait," Mom said. "If your family put the cap on originally, why don't you put it back? That will be safer, right?"

"It's not that simple," Tamsin said. "Kimmy has three open connections at the moment that we're unable to break and the way her power is unbridled, it would be like trying to stop a waterfall with a bucket."

"That's—" Mom rubbed at her forehead with a grimace. "Oh, Kimmy."

Alex was peering at Tamsin, deep in thought. She tilted her head at him curiously.

"If you haven't told your parents about any of this," he asked her slowly, "where exactly do they think you are right now?"

"An internship for college?" Tamsin said sheepishly.

He and Mom exchanged a look that said Tamsin would be answering a few more questions later.

"I'd like to know more about this evil witch," Mrs. Manning said, hands clasped together under her chin. "You're telling me we have a *serial killer* right here in Basbridge?"

My teeth clacked together as my mouth slammed shut over *that* suggestion. A serial—no. But maybe? "I mean . . ." Depending on how you looked at it. "Kind of?"

"Hot dog," Mr. Kingsley whispered. "You should have led with that, kid."

"This is just like that podcast my friend Marg introduced me to," Mrs. Manning said, excitement creeping into her voice. "*Small-Town Secrets*. I was hooked from the first episode." She held up her hand to whisper behind it across the table to Mr. Kingsley. "It turned out the killer was the funeral home director."

"Hmm." Mr. Kingsley said a lot with one little noise as they both side-eyed me.

Devon hopped his chair around the table to Mrs. Manning's side. "Tell me more."

"Okay, listen." I waved my hands in the air as if I could brush off the nonsense and get us refocused. "Why don't we—"

"Let Mrs. Manning tell everyone about that podcast while I speak with Kimmy," Mom said, cutting me off with a pointed look. Her chair grated across the floor as she stood and jerked her chin toward the hallway. *"Alone."*

Chapter Seventeen

I followed her out into the hall and all the way to her office, where she shut the door behind us. Mom paced in front of her desk while I stood there in silence. Me speaking first didn't seem like the most helpful move.

After a few minutes, she finally stopped and faced me. "We talked about this," she said. "We agreed that you were going to leave it alone. You knew how dangerous it was. You *knew*! And you went ahead and did it."

"I thought—"

"You didn't think! If you'd been thinking, you wouldn't have tried in the first place," Mom said, scrubbing a hand down her face. "I still can't believe it."

"But listen for a second," I said. "Please." If she would

let me explain what it was like, how I *knew* that I had to push through, she'd understand. "The power was guiding me," I said. "I knew I could help—with Devon. I had to try."

"I don't care about the why," Mom cried. "I care that you *tried*. Your grandmother told you what happened to your father and you still tried. You could have *died*, Kimmy!" She blinked back tears as she yelled. "Did you think about that?"

Alex slipped quietly into the room and came to stand beside her, wrapping an arm around her shoulders. "Maybe we should take a break," he said quietly.

I didn't want that. I didn't want to leave things like this. "Mom, I'm sorry," I said. "I didn't—I was sure I could do it."

She sighed, leaning into Alex for a moment. "So was your father."

"Your mother and I only want you to be safe," Alex said. He gave a rueful nod toward the kitchen. "Obviously, that's a complicated thing right now, but it'll be easier if you talk to us."

Mom took a deep breath, giving herself a shake. "No more lies, Kimmy," she said. "Or hiding things. I know your grandmother taught you to keep everything about the power close, but that stops now. We're *all* a part of this family and you can't keep things from us."

"We might not have magic," Alex said. "But we can help and support you."

"And tell you when you're going too far," Mom said. "Let's be honest. That's why you kept it a secret, because you knew we'd stop you from trying to Wake Devon."

I kept my mouth shut, not wanting to get myself in any more trouble.

Because she was right.

I hadn't wanted to be stopped and part of me wasn't sorry.

"I still can't believe you did it," Mom said, eyeing me thoughtfully. "Why were you able to break the cap when your father—" She shook her head. "How was it possible?"

"Has there been anything different with your power lately?" Alex asked. "Any changes when you use it?"

No more lying, I reminded myself. I told them about how much stronger my power was since Grandma died and the strange tugs. The glowing hands and incident in the prep room were a little trickier to explain.

Mom dragged a hand through her hair. "Bev never mentioned *anything* like that to me," she said. "Neither did your father."

"She never said anything to me, either." I shrugged. "I've been reading through the journals, but I haven't found anything yet." That gave me an idea. "I think maybe it would go faster if I had some help?"

"You'd let us read the Jones family journals?" Mom raised an extremely skeptical eyebrow at me.

"We would be honored," Alex said smoothly. "Maybe they'll give us some helpful information on getting through this . . . evil witch issue as well."

"Afterward," Mom added, "we'll discuss how very grounded you are."

I'd been waiting for that.

"Tamsin has a half a plan for the whole evil witch thing," I offered. The spell had to count for something.

"Half a plan is always better than no plan," Alex declared as he led the way back to the kitchen.

Mrs. Manning perked up at the table when we returned. "We've been comparing notes," she said. "Since we're here, we might as well assist. I was a reference librarian way back when, so I'm used to sifting through information, and Eddie here was a detective! Isn't that handy?"

Mr. Kingsley coughed into his fist and blushed. "Uh, just an insurance investigator, remember? But I know a clue when I see one!"

"We were thinking we could use the kitchen as home

base," Tamsin said. "It has a nice big table with enough space for everyone to work. We need to compile all of our information."

"That makes sense," Mom said, getting into it now that we were officially in planning mode. "We were going to look through the family journals to see if there's anything helpful in there."

"Excellent idea," Tamsin agreed. "The more we know about Kimmy's power, the better, since this is all intertwined."

"We could use that wall to make one of those murder boards like they do on TV," Mrs. Manning exclaimed.

Everyone started talking at once after that, chipping in ideas about things to focus on and who could do what.

"We haven't been properly introduced," Alex was saying to Mrs. Manning. "I'm Alex Yoo, Julia's husband and Kimmy's stepfather."

"Please call me Paulette." She reached out to shake Alex's hand.

"You can all call me Ed," Mr. Kingsley added.

With all of the organized chaos unfolding in front of me, it took a minute to realize what was missing. Or rather, who.

"Where's Devon?" I asked, but no one heard me over

the din. "Hey!" I yelled. "Where did Devon go?"

Everyone went quiet and looked around the room.

"He was here a minute ago," Tamsin said. "I swear."

"We have to find him," I said, heading for the kitchen door when Mom swiftly stepped in my way.

"Absolutely not," she said.

"We can't leave him *alone* out there," I said. "The witch wants him!"

"Exactly why it's too dangerous for you to go," Mom said. "*We* will go and look for him." She gestured at herself and Alex. "The rest of you will stay here."

"Not to step on any toes," Tamsin piped up. "But I should probably go. What with the magic element involved."

"Fine." Mom waved a hand through the air. "Tamsin will go with one of us—"

"He's my responsibility," I said firmly.

"And you're mine," Mom countered.

I bit back a groan. She wasn't going to listen and arguing was wasting more time. The witch could swoop in and grab Devon any moment. What if she found a way to sever my connection to him and was able to take back his life force?

We might never find him.

Reaching for the power, I breathed a sigh of relief when I found our connection intact. Stretched, but still running strong. At least I could be sure he was alive out there. Somewhere.

Tug, tug, tug.

Wait, that was it. The *connection.*

"I should be the one to go," I said, rushing to make my case before Mom could shut it down. "We're connected through my power and it feels different now that he's farther away. I think I can use it to track him down."

The closer we got, the stronger the connection.

"It's not a terrible idea," Tamsin said, shooting an apologetic look at Mom. "The quicker we find Devon, the better. If Kimmy's confident she can locate him this way, it'll be more efficient than driving around looking for him with no idea where to start."

"I can take them," Alex said and I had to stop myself from cheering. "If it doesn't work, we'll come right back and drop Kimmy off before looking again."

That could be a distant plan B. My plan was going to work.

Tug, tug, tug.

I was sure of it.

Mom and Alex looked at each other, having some kind of silent discussion before Mom finally turned to me, holding up a firm finger. "You will do exactly as Alex says and you will not argue when it's time to come home. No matter what."

"Yes, agreed, let's go!" I ran for the back door, waiting for Tamsin and Alex to follow.

"We'll start bringing down the journals and reading through them," Mom said. "Hopefully, we'll have something to go on by the time you get back."

"Sounds good." Pushing Tamsin and Alex out the door, I hurried them along to the garage. Once Tamsin was settled in the front seat and I was in the back, Alex backed out and down the driveway. Where he stopped.

"Alex, come on—"

"Left or right, Kimmy?" he said. "You're the one with the tracking system."

Oh, yeah. I tuned into the connection, trying to decide which way had a stronger vibe. Left? Or right?

Tug, tug, tug.

"Right," I said. Alex turned and I tried to sense our next direction.

It wasn't a turn, but the actual destination that became clear to me. Now that my panic had died down, I realized I knew exactly where he was. "Tamsin." I reached over the back of her seat. "May I see your phone?"

She was instantly suspicious. "What for?"

"To see where Devon went."

"You said your connection could tell you that," Alex said. "And you promised no more lying—"

"That wasn't a lie!" I made grabby hands at Tamsin's phone. "But this will be faster."

She handed it over warily. "You're sure you know what you're looking for?"

"Yes." I searched addresses in Basbridge under the name Sawyer. "Devon told me."

A few times.

Luck was on my side when only one result came up. I read out the address to Alex and he turned the next corner.

"Where are we headed?" he asked.

"His house."

Chapter Eighteen

Minutes later, we were driving down River Road and parking a few spots down from number twenty-five. A cute black-and-white house with a bright garden and a bike lying on the grass.

Devon sat on the curb across the street, arms over his knees.

"Let me go talk to him?" I asked and Alex nodded.

"We're sticking close by though," he said. "Just in case."

The three of us got out of the car, but Alex and Tamsin hung back while I crossed the distance to Devon, taking a seat beside him.

His hair was messy and he was sweating like he'd run

the whole way over. And his eyes were red. Like he'd been crying. He didn't look at me when I sat down. Just kept his gaze trained on the house. "Well," he said with a sniff. "I figured one thing out."

"What?"

"My family has no idea who I am," Devon said, voice breaking. "I knocked on the door and my mom answered. 'May I help you?' That's what she said. That's it." He sniffed. "I told her I had the wrong address."

"Devon—"

"Devon Sawyer doesn't exist," he said, turning his attention back to the house.

"You exist," I said, knocking my shoulder into his. "You're here."

I'd made sure of that.

"I wish I wasn't." Devon shook his head. "I wish you never brought me back."

He didn't know what he was saying. "That would have left you with the witch—"

"I'd rather be left with her than be here and know what it's like to be erased."

"No, listen, after we defeat the witch, Tamsin can find a way to break the memory spell," I said.

Devon scoffed bitterly. "So?" He faced me again,

eyebrows raised. "You don't know what'll happen with our connection after the witch is stopped. This could all end with me being dead again. *Dead* dead. Unless you know how to use your powers to stop that from happening."

He was right. I didn't know what was going to happen. And if he was supposed to go back to rest, I couldn't use my powers to stop it.

I *hated* that. More than I ever had before. I couldn't bring myself to say the words, but Devon figured it out from my silence.

"Yeah, didn't think so," he whispered, burying his face in his arms.

I racked my brain, searching for something that could fix this. Some way to help.

"Maybe," I began, ". . . maybe I *could* turn you into a zombie."

Absolute silence.

Then his shoulders started to shake and Devon lifted his head with a snort. "I thought you didn't do that."

"I'd give it a shot as, like, a last resort," I said with a shrug.

Devon laughed and I cracked a grin. "All right," he said. "Good to know we have a plan Z if all else fails."

"That's the spirit," I said, swaying to bump gently into

his side. He leaned in, giggling with me until he stopped abruptly.

A ragged breath came out instead.

"Devon." I turned to him, wondering if he'd let me give him a hug, and found myself face-to-face with a pair of bright, glowing blue eyes.

"*Tamsin!*" I yelled. This was definitely a backup-required situation.

"Kimmy!" Alex came running up with Tamsin on his heels. He pulled me away from Devon, standing between us while Tamsin rooted through her bag, cursing.

"Come on, come on, where *is it*?"

Devon stood up with a jerk, mouth moving into a grim imitation of a grin. "He's mine," the same raspy woman's voice as before breathed out.

"Stay back," Alex said, holding up a hand as Devon crept closer. "Kimmy, go to the car."

"I'm not—"

"Do as I say!" Alex yelled.

In the split second that he turned to look at me, Devon reached out and grabbed his wrist. Alex whipped his head back, trying to yank himself free.

"*You're* mine," the voice said.

All of a sudden, Alex's face went slack.

The voice laughed, a rough, creaky thing.

"Stop! What are you doing to him?" I waved my hand in front of Alex's face, but there was no response. "Tamsin!"

"I'm working on it!" she snarled.

Devon's hand glowed blue and the color started to drain out of Alex's face. Like the witch was using Devon as a—a conduit for her powers. She was trying to steal Alex's spark!

"No! No, no, no!" I clutched at Alex's other arm. Maybe I could grab on to his spark before the witch pulled it free.

But then Alex's legs were giving out and I couldn't *concentrate*—

"Duck!" Tamsin yelled and I crouched down as a little packet sailed over my head and hit Devon square in the face, exploding in a flurry of powder.

He immediately let go and Alex fell to the ground. Devon started coughing, scraping at his face. "What the heck was that?" he yelled, thankfully in his normal voice.

"I call it the Be Gone Bomb. I made it myself," Tamsin said, a proud grin on her face as she swooped in to help me get Alex to his feet. "My own special formula designed to disrupt negative energies. Pretty good, eh?"

Devon hunched over, sneezing five times in a row and Tamsin frowned.

"Still gotta work out that black pepper to mullein ratio, though." She fished a package of wet wipes out of her bag and started dabbing at his face.

"I think the delivery system could use some work, too." Devon groaned.

"And maybe keep them somewhere more accessible?" I said. That had been way too close.

"Oof, my head," Alex moaned, rubbing a hand against his forehead as he squinted at us. "Everyone okay?"

"Us? What about you?" I waved my hand in front of his face. "How many fingers?"

"That test doesn't work if you move them that fast," he said, gently pressing my hand back down. "I have a headache and I'm a little woozy, but okay, I think?"

My stomach dropped at the sight of a few new gray hairs at his temple. How much had she managed to steal from him? Was he actually okay? "Tamsin, can you check him over? Make sure he's all there with no leftovers from the witch?"

"That's a good idea," she said, guiding Devon forward as I kept a hand on Alex. "Let's get in the car and off the street. I don't think we should draw any more attention to ourselves."

She grabbed a water bottle once we were back in the car and helped Devon rinse the rest of his face. Then she did a quick check of Alex to confirm he was in the clear.

"The Be Gone Bomb disruption is only temporary," she said. "I'm not sure how long the effects will last. If she can use Devon as a conduit for her powers now, we have to be ready to dose him again."

"How many more of those things do you have?" Alex asked and she nodded.

"Only three, but I have a stash of supplies in my car," she said. "I can make more once we get back to the funeral home."

The funeral home. Where Ed and Paulette were. I leapt forward, grabbing on to the front seat. "Ed and Paulette!"

"What about them?" Tamsin reared back, my flailing hands narrowly missing smacking her in the chin.

"*The witch!*" I yelled. "She can connect with them the same way she does with Devon, right?"

Alex twisted around in his seat. "What about the house protections?"

"Since she's not physically there, they might not be effective," Tamsin gasped.

"And Mom's home alone with them," I said, prodding at Alex's shoulder.

"Everyone, buckle up," he said, turning on the car and peeling away from the curb. "Tamsin, call Julia."

I tried to put my seatbelt on, but my shaking hands kept missing. Devon reached over and helped me put the buckle into place. I gave him a short nod in thanks, falling back in my seat.

My head was swimming again.

"Her phone keeps going to voicemail," Tamsin announced.

"Try again," Alex said, terse as he gripped the wheel on a tight turn.

A jaunty ringtone filled the car. "It's her! She's calling!" Tamsin exclaimed.

"Answer it!" all three of us yelled.

"I'm trying!" She swiped a finger across the screen and hit speaker. "Julia?"

"Tamsin! Where are you?" Mom's voice was tight. "Is everyone okay?"

"We're on our way," Alex called out. "I can't explain at the moment, but where are you in the house? You need to get somewhere safe."

"What? Uh, I'm—I'm in Bev's room," Mom said. "I was grabbing the last of the journals."

"Are you alone?" Tamsin asked into the phone.

"Yes?"

"Good," Alex said. "Lock the door and push whatever

you can in front of it. Do not let Ed or Paulette in."

"Alex, *what is going on?*"

"Please, Julia!" he said. Tamsin held the phone out so he could lean toward the speaker. "We'll be there soon."

After an agonizing pause, Mom said, "Okay. I'll lock the door, but let me know when you're here so I can help with . . . whatever this is." She ended the call and Tamsin shoved her phone back in her bag.

"You have those bomb things handy?" Alex asked Tamsin, and she nodded.

"And I've got the rest of the wet wipes," Devon said.

Alex headed for our street. "Let's go see what we're dealing with."

Chapter Nineteen

The four of us stood on the front porch, bracing ourselves to go in.

Tamsin had texted Mom, but she wasn't answering.

Alex eyed the door grimly. "I think you kids should stay out here."

And leave them without anyone to watch their backs?

"No way," I said, turning to Devon for assistance, and he stared at me blankly before catching on.

"Oh, you want me to— Nooooo." He plopped down on one of the wicker chairs. "No, thank you. I'm good sitting this one out and steering clear of the possession zone."

"Pretty sure that's not how it works," I said.

"In any case . . . " Tamsin dug through her bag and

handed me one of the Be Gone Bombs. "Keep that handy in case she comes through Devon again."

"You think she can control more than one person at a time?" That would be . . . real bad.

"I think better safe than sorry," she said. "Aim for his chest, that's where the energy is most concentrated."

Devon scowled. "Why'd you hit me in the face, then?"

Tamsin coughed and looked away, muttering something.

"Hmm?" He leaned forward. "What was that?"

"I said I missed!" She threw her hands up, bag rattling at her side. "My bad, okay?"

Devon made an indignant noise and Alex sliced a hand through the air.

"Enough!" he barked, making us all jump. "We're wasting time. Tamsin and I are going in. Kimmy, stay here. *Please.*" It was the please that had me caving.

"Be safe," I whispered as they went inside, closing the door quietly behind themselves.

Devon settled into his chair and I crept closer to the door.

"What are you doing?" He tilted his head back, watching me with an unimpressed glare.

"Listening," I said. "See if I can tell how it's going." I pressed an ear against the wood, waiting for any cries of pain or screams of terror or . . . pepper-induced sneezing.

"Anything?" Devon asked, leaning over the armrest.

I shushed him.

No screams, but there was something.

Footsteps?

The door swung open and a hand latched on to my arm, pulling me inside. All I heard was a cut-off *"Hey!"* from Devon before the door slammed shut.

Paulette gripped my arm with one hand while the other pressed my shoulder back into the wood. Her eyes glowed bright blue.

I lifted my free hand, ready to bean her with the Be Gone Bomb, only to realize it wasn't there. I thunked my head against the door, cursing myself for dropping it.

Now I had nothing to fight off Paulette with.

"Little witch," the witch's voice said, twisting Paulette's lips in a sharp smile.

Oh, good, she wanted to chat.

The door opened a crack as Devon tried to push his way in and Paulette slammed it shut again, reaching around me to lock it. She was disturbingly strong. The witch was gaining better control with each possession and I didn't want to stick around to find out what tricks she'd learned.

I tried to duck around her, but she held firm.

"Where are Alex and Tamsin?" It couldn't be a good sign that there was no one else in sight.

"With the other one," Paulette said, jerking a nod at the closed doors of the main viewing room. The muffled sounds of a crash rang out and I hoped that didn't mean we were down *two* Be Gone Bombs.

Maybe Devon had found the other one and would remember the kitchen entrance existed. Until then, I needed another way to take down Paulette. Gently.

I really didn't want to have to tackle an eighty-something-year-old.

Think, Kimmy, think.

The hand gripping my arm started to glow blue and an icy chill clawed its way through my veins. Was this what it had felt like for Devon?

For Grandma?

"Your power," the witch said. Paulette's eyes closed as she sighed deeply. "Delicious."

I tugged on her hold. "Get off of me."

"Shame to kill you." The witch leaned in to whisper in my face. "When I should thank you. Connections. Conduits. You could help me reach further. Live forever."

"Why would I help you?" I shuddered. "I don't hurt people."

A deep, gravelly laugh at that. "You think? I'm not the only one with stolen—"

Thwack!

A cloud of powder enveloped Paulette as a Be Gone Bomb hit her square in the back.

"Yes!" Devon cheered from his spot in the hallway before his face went white. "I just threw a magical bomb at a senior citizen. Paulette! Are you okay?"

"Hey, are you still there?" I waved my hand in front of Paulette, trying to clear away some of the eye-watering cloud. She was coughing and blinking as tears ran down her cheeks. "I'm not the only one with stolen *what?*"

"What, dear?" Paulette croaked, peering at me with her very normal brown eyes.

"Ugh, Devon!" Worst timing ever. "You couldn't have waited *five seconds?*"

"I'm not hearing a thank-you," Devon snarked at me as he came over and handed Paulette a few wet wipes.

"Thanks." I sighed.

The doors to the viewing room slid open and Alex and Tamsin appeared, leading a coughing and hacking Ed.

"I refuse to believe you haven't got a better delivery system for that," Ed rasped.

Devon nodded emphatically at Tamsin as he brought the wet wipes over to Ed.

"What happened?" Paulette asked, looking around the room. "Why are we—"

"Wait, where's Mom?" I hadn't heard her voice once. "Is she still upstairs? Did you see her? Did one of you *do something*—"

"Sweetie, I have no memory of anything that's gone on since shortly after you left," Paulette said. "Last I saw your mother, she was heading up for the last of the journals."

I ran for the stairs, taking them two at a time as Alex thumped along behind me. "Mom?" I called out as we hit the landing. "Mom!"

Grandma's door was closed and locked.

Alex knocked on the door. "Julia?" he said. "Are you in there?"

"It's safe now." Relatively speaking. I tried jiggling the handle again. "Mom, open up!"

The door flew open. Mom appeared in the doorway, hair messy and eyes red. She stared at me and Alex, her mouth opening and closing once as she shook her head. Pressing a hand against her forehead, she walked back inside the room and stood in front of Grandma's bed.

I snuck a peek at Alex, but he looked as confused as I was. We followed her inside.

The room was a mess.

Grandma's bed was covered in loose papers, all with different handwriting on them. A few journals were spread out as well. The bookshelf that had held the whole collection was lying on its side with the bottom shelf half off. Mom caught me staring at it.

"It was empty," she said. "I thought it would be the easiest thing to block the door with and then I was going to climb out the window onto the porch roof so I could meet you outside." She waved a hand at the collection on the bed. "The bottom came apart when I tipped it over and all of *this* was hidden in there."

"What is it?" I moved closer to get a better look.

"I can't—" Mom pressed shaky fingers to her lips. "I should have asked more questions," she whispered. "I should have demanded to read the journals myself. I should have—ugh! How could they *do this*?"

"Who did what?" I demanded, trying not to be snippy, but today had already been full of unexplainable weirdness and I'd kind of reached my limit.

Alex picked up one of the journals and flipped it open. He let out a soft noise as he read the first page, quickly passing it over to me.

It was one of Grandma Bev's.

"I've been looking everywhere for those!" Why would she have hidden them in the bookshelf? "Who do those belong to?" I pointed at the other journals but got distracted by one of the pieces of paper tossed beside them. It had a ragged edge, like it had been torn.

The handwriting looked familiar.

"This is from Dad's journals," I said, picking it up. I looked back over the papers spread out on the bed. "These are the missing pages from all of the journals. Who did this?"

"You know who did it," Mom said, fury simmering at the edge of every word.

The only person who could have done it.

Grandma.

But why?

Skimming over the page from Dad's journal, I tried to find a clue. Anything. The entry was about how he "didn't know how to tell Julia the truth because she hadn't grown up with it and would never understand."

"I can't believe they—" Mom clenched her hands into fists in front of her and let out a frustrated yell. "To hide it from me? From *you*? It should have been your *choice*. How dare they—"

"Mom!" I dropped Grandma's journal and Dad's page onto the bed so I could grab her hands. "Hide *what*?"

"The cost," she blurted out, gripping my hands tight. "Of using your power."

Devon's questions from yesterday came back to me.

And Tamsin's explanation on the finite nature of power.

The *witch* saying she wasn't the only one with stolen . . . something.

What was so horrible that Grandma and Dad kept it hidden?

"Do we hurt people?" I whispered. Everything inside me screamed that couldn't be possible.

Tug, tug, TUG.

I wanted to believe it was good, but how could I trust that now?

TUG, TUG, TUG.

"Not other people." Mom shook her head roughly. "You." Her hold on my fingers turned almost painful. "Every time you Wake someone, you use up a part of your own life force."

Chapter Twenty

I could understand the words she was saying, but that didn't mean they made sense.

"Use up? Like—"

"Like an energy transfer." She closed her eyes briefly as a pained expression crossed over her face. "Five minutes keeping someone alive is five minutes off your life."

I shook my head. That wasn't right. "No, I don't—where does it say all of this?" I grabbed Grandma's journal. "What page? Grandma wouldn't keep something like that a secret."

"It's on every single one of these pages," Mom said as she sank down to sit on the bed. "They're all from different journals, including your dad's. She tore out every reference and hid them away with her own journals."

I cleared a space and sat down beside her. "But she had to be planning on telling me eventually," I said. "Like she did with—with Dad's death."

"She certainly never told me," Mom said softly, her voice going thick. "And your father didn't see fit to, either. I never in a million years would have thought he'd keep something like this from me. That she'd keep it from *us*." Alex moved to Mom's other side and she leaned into him, shaking her head.

Maybe it was like with the cap and Grandma had been waiting until I could handle the truth and fully understand the dangers.

Except I hadn't fully understood, had I? Because this— this was the real danger. The reason for the cap. And now the cap was *gone* and I was using my life to power three other people. The realization left me dizzy as I pictured my energy flowing out to the others.

"Devon," I said. "Ed and Paulette."

"I know." She squeezed my hand. "You have to break those connections."

"I've tried—"

"You broke through the cap when no one else could," Mom whispered urgently, eyes tearing up. "You have to be able to do this, too. Try. Please."

"Julia," Alex said. "Shouldn't we talk to them first? They're in the kitchen. Let's go down and—"

"They're *stealing* her life. Even one minute is too much." Mom broke away, standing up to pace the short width of Grandma's room. "This is going to *kill* you, Kimmy, and I refuse to waste time talking it out when we can put a stop to it right now."

"I can't," I repeated. "And even if I could, I don't think saying goodbye would be a *waste of time*."

She crossed her arms tightly around herself, face pinched. "They're all nice people, Kimmy, but I'm sorry. The only person who can be saved here is you."

"I told you—"

"Try again!"

"I don't know *how!*"

A kernel of resentment popped up deep inside my chest. That Grandma could leave me before I was prepared for any of this. Even if she didn't mean to.

"Well, I'm not going to stop until we figure that out," Mom said, gathering up the pages and journals into a loose pile in her arms. "The answer has to be somewhere in this mess." She headed for the door. "Tamsin!"

"Wait." I dove for the pile in her hands and started digging through it, grabbing the pages with Dad's writing and Grandma's journals. "I just—I need to read these for myself," I said, settling them in a neat stack. "You can get started on the rest of it. I promise I'll be fast."

"We can't afford detours, Kimmy," Mom said. "Not with this."

"Ten minutes," I begged. I didn't think arguing the fact that it was *my* time to waste would get me anywhere.

"Fine. Do what you want." Managing an angry shrug even with her arms full, Mom walked out of the room. "It's the Jones way."

"Mom!"

"Julia—" Alex called after her, but she didn't come back. He paused in the doorway and rapped a knuckle against the wood with a sigh. "She's scared," he said quietly. "We both are." He shot a quick glance in Mom's direction before hitting me with a solemn look. "I know you want answers, but this is your *life*, Kimmy."

He walked away, leaving me alone in Grandma's room.

I knew the clock was ticking, but I needed a moment with Dad and Grandma. To read their words without an audience.

"Okay," I whispered, sitting down on her bed. "Help me understand."

Flipping through Dad's pages, I read as quickly as I could.

Grandma had told him about the cap and the cost of our power shortly after he'd started training at the age of twelve. He freaked out about it for a couple of pages and then the fear fell away. With each passing entry, he grew more fascinated with the scope of our magic and what we could do.

When Grandpa became ill, Dad started researching other forms of magic. Searching for other ways to fuel our power so he could help Grandpa without hurting himself.

Then Grandpa died and I was born and Dad—pretty much threw himself into his experiments, like Grandma said.

She never told me, though, that he did it for us. Me, Mom, and Grandma.

He was determined to break the cap and find a way to use his power without draining himself so he could save us if something ever happened.

If.

I fought the urge to crumple the pages in my hands. Part of me understood. If I'd been with Grandma when she died and if I could have saved her, I'd have done it.

But this was—he put himself in danger for something that might not have ever happened. We all could have lived regular-length, normal (for us) lives and he could have been there *with* us. Instead of dying himself.

One of the last entries was him admitting that he

didn't want to talk to Grandma or fill Mom in on everything because he didn't want them to stop him.

I set down his pages and scrubbed at my eyes, trying to will away the sting. Kind of understood now why Mom was so mad.

At him and at me.

We'd both forged ahead, ignoring the consequences of our actions and how they'd affect *everyone* in our family.

What had Grandma's plan been in all of this?

I picked up her journals. It took some digging, but I found entries that started after Dad passed away.

This is my fault.

I should have kept a closer eye on him. I should have known that Nathan would never be content to stick to a boundary. Not when he always wanted to help. To fix.

Nathan and I talked about the dangers of trying to break the cap. I thought he understood. I thought I taught him better.

I gave him too much space.

~~I should have known~~

~~Why didn't I see~~

This is my fault.

Most of the entries after that were about her helping Mom raise me and working the funeral home together. She mentioned hiding everything from the family journals that talked about the cost of our power so that Mom and I wouldn't find out if we went snooping. As if we'd *dare*. She didn't want me to learn about it until it was time. Or Mom to discover the truth and take me away.

But it sounded like Grandma *was* planning on telling me?

I flipped through until I found the journal with entries about her starting my training.

It's time for Kimmy to start training and—

I'm scared.

Julia is too and she doesn't even know

I'm attempting to manage both our fears and make a plan at the same time. There is a process for introducing children in our family to their power and beginning their training. It failed Nathan, but was that because of the process or because I was his teacher?

I don't want to make the same mistakes, but what changes are the right ones?

Telling Kimmy about the cap will mean telling her about her father's death. Which will lead to a discussion about the cost of our power. So much information for one conversation. I don't want to overwhelm her.

When it comes time to tell her about the cap, I'll see how she takes it. If she needs a bit of space before hearing the rest, I'll give it to her. A few days won't hurt.

I'll keep a closer eye on her. I'll tell her everything. I know what to look for now and I'll keep her safe.

I closed the journal and set it down carefully beside me on the papers.

She wanted to tell me. She'd planned to be here for all of my training. To walk me through everything. It wasn't Grandma's fault a witch got in the way.

But she'd kept secrets. Put everything on herself. Her journal said it all—"*I'll* keep a closer eye on her. *I'll* keep her safe." Just like Dad and his "*I'll* be the one to break the cap." If either one of them had let Mom in, who knew how differently things would have played out.

I had to be the one to change. No more trying to do things on my own. I might be the only Jones left, but I wasn't actually alone. The only way we were going to get through this was as a team.

Grabbing the pages and Grandma's journal, I headed downstairs.

Chapter Twenty-One

Everyone was gathered around the table, engrossed in the journals. A half-full platter of sandwiches sat on the counter with a small pile of plates beside it.

Alex saw me first. "We made some food," he said, hopping up to grab me a plate. "And filled them in," he added quietly as he handed it over. Devon sent me a heavy look before returning to poking at Tamsin's tablet.

"Find anything yet?" I asked. Mom pulled out a chair for me in silent invitation. Sliding in beside her, I leaned into her side and she gave me a little hug.

"I believe Tamsin is on to something," Paulette said around a mouthful of egg salad.

"Stand by," Tamsin murmured, holding up a finger as she kept reading.

Five more minutes passed with her muttering to herself and making notes on a scrap of paper before finally looking up. "This is actually quite fascinating," she said brightly.

A quick glance around the table had her lowering the wattage a bit.

"Or it would be if we weren't under the threat of a murderous witch and on a time crunch," she said, clearing her throat as she tapped the pages in front of her. "These are the two earliest journals—from back in the 1870s."

"The ones Grandma hid under the bookshelf." With her own journals and all the missing pages from the other journals. They *had* to have something useful in them.

"They belonged to sisters, Edith and Irene Jones," Tamsin said. "Your family line is descended from Irene. Their whole family had healing magic—"

"Like the evil witch?" Devon cut in.

"Yes! Cecilia West. Good memory." Tamsin pointed a finger at him. "Back to Edith and Irene." She grabbed a marker and stood up, moving to the wall of paper Paulette had set up on the far side of the kitchen.

"She's using the murder board," Paulette whispered, clapping her hands in quiet excitement.

"Here we have the Jones family," Tamsin said, writing the names up on the left side and adding an extra one. Clara. "There were more of them, but we're focusing on the sisters. The family had healing magic. They would take the curative energies from plants or crystals or whatever natural item they were working with and bind it to the person who was ill, which would fix them. Most of the time."

"But you can't heal everything," Ed said.

"No, you can't." Tamsin circled Clara's name. "This became a problem when the youngest sister became ill with scarlet fever and the other two were not able to help her." She underlined Irene's name on the chart. "Irene's grief twisted her power. Her need to cure her sister was so great that she brought Clara back from the dead."

The first one in the family to do so, according to Tamsin's research.

"When did it start to go wrong?" I asked.

"Pretty much immediately," Tamsin said. "Edith wrote that Irene's power kept expanding, bringing back the recently dead and healing people from greater distances over the course of a few days."

Without touch. Like my power jumping to Wake Paulette.

"Did she pass out like Kimmy did?" Devon asked.

Mom and Alex slowly turned to pin me with identical unimpressed looks.

"We talked about that already," I said. "Didn't we? I'm sure we did. Let's hear the rest of the story."

"Irene did pass out," Tamsin said. "A few times, according to Edith, until she, uh, died."

Well, that wasn't encouraging.

"The power kept drawing from her in increasing amounts until her life force burnt up," Tamsin continued. "And when she died . . . so did everyone else she'd brought back."

The kitchen was silent as we took that in.

Tamsin coughed and tapped her marker against her hand. "So then the problem was—"

"There were *more problems*?" Devon exclaimed.

"Mostly the one . . . well, two," Tamsin said. "First they had to cover everything up, which was a pretty big job."

Probably took more than a few memory spells.

"But also, Edith wrote that as Irene's children grew older, their power manifested in the same boundless way that their mother's had twisted into. Magic runs through a family's veins like blood and keeps you connected." Tamsin drew three stick figures under Irene and added swirling lines flowing between them all. "Irene's alteration or mutation, whatever you want to call it, affected the whole line."

"Grandma told me it's like the roots of a tree," I said. "The same power that spread through her traveled through me."

"Exactly," Tamsin said. "Edith was caring for Irene's children at that point and called in my family to put the cap on."

"Well," I said, slumping down in my chair. "This was a fun history lesson."

"Kimmy." Mom reached out to grab my knee. Voice short. "Don't." She looked over at Tamsin. "How does any of this help us?"

For the first time since I'd sat down, Tamsin fell out of excited teacher mode. She pressed her lips together for a moment before speaking again. "It helps because now I understand what's going on with Kimmy's power," she said. "That twist from Irene essentially turned it into wild magic. It's like it has a mind of its own."

"That's why I couldn't stop it from Waking Ed and Paulette," I said, remembering how it had surged out of my control down in the prep room.

Tamsin nodded. "It's too powerful," she said. "And I think—" She dropped eye contact to stare at the table and cleared her throat. "I think that's why you haven't been able to break the connections with Devon, Ed, and Paulette. Why you *won't* be able to. It's—"

"Why can't you put the cap back on?" Mom demanded. "Or use your magic to break it?"

"Kimmy's magic is *much* stronger than mine at the moment," Tamsin said. "But what I'm trying to say is that the strength of her magic is not the only problem. It's the links." She shook her head, tapping her marker against her hand. "The witch called Devon a *conduit*."

I nodded. "When she was using him to try and drain Alex's spark. She reached through him with her power."

"Right," Tamsin said and turned back to the board with her marker in hand. Mom reached out to touch her elbow.

"Please, no more diagrams," she said. "Just tell me what you think is happening so we can stop it."

"I think that Kimmy's power is also using these three as conduits, but it's trying to get through to the witch to heal *her*," Tamsin said.

"How do you heal someone who's a hundred years past their expiration date?" Devon asked.

"I think the point is that I *can't*," I said and Mom let out a hurt little noise.

"But it'll kill you trying to do it," she whispered.

"Where does that leave us?" Alex asked, grasping Mom's hand in his.

"There's my spell." Tamsin capped her marker with a snap. "Once the witch's power is erased, Kimmy's power would stop searching it out and we'd have a shot at resetting the cap."

"This is the spell that you haven't even tested yet? There has to be a safer way," Mom protested. "Something to stop it from Kimmy's side."

Tamsin sighed. "I wish there was—"

"What if . . . ," Alex spoke up hesitantly, "we used your spell on Kimmy instead?"

Erase *my* power?

TUG, TUG, TUG!

All of my alarm bells were going off. "No! Wait—"

"You said the spell was specifically for the witch." Mom ignored me as she stared intensely at Tamsin. "Would you be able to make one for Kimmy?"

"I think I could," Tamsin said, apology coloring every word as she avoided *my* stare. "I have everything here, but I'd need a hair from Kimmy for the biomarkers. It'll take me a little time to set up."

"Anything you need," Mom said firmly.

"We're not going to talk about this?" I turned to her.

"Having no power is better than being dead," she snapped.

"Julia," Alex murmured, nodding discreetly at Ed, Paulette, and Devon when Mom looked his way.

The three people who *were* going to be dead at the end of this plan.

Again.

"Sorry." Mom cursed quietly as she massaged the deep line forming between her brows. "I'm *sorry*," she said. "I know what this means for all of you and I wish—I wish it didn't."

Her words rested heavily in the silence of the kitchen.

Ed was the first one to speak. "I wasn't ready to go," he said. "But I don't want to stick around if it means taking Kimmy's life before she's had a chance to live it. It is what it is."

Paulette nodded. "I agree with Ed," she said. "I won't sacrifice Kimmy to give myself more time. And these connections all need to be broken somehow if we're going to stop the witch."

Devon stared down at the table, not saying anything and I couldn't blame him.

I knew when I went to Wake him that I'd be putting him back to rest, but I thought it would be over and done with in a few minutes. Like it always had been. No time for talking or jokes or . . . making friends.

I was stealing his life away from him all over again.

My stomach rolled as Alex stood up. "Should we go down to the prep room? That might make this easier." Chairs scraped across the floor as Ed, Paulette, and Mom joined him.

How could they be so matter-of-fact about it? So *clinical*.

Devon met my eyes across the table.

This was all wrong. It wasn't how we were supposed to do things.

"Wait," I called out. Tamsin had said she needed a little time so I was going to take it. We had to get this one part right. "We have to do last wishes."

Chapter Twenty-Two

"Kimmy." Mom gave me a warning look, but I pushed ahead because if we had to do this, I wasn't going to skip any steps.

I could give my new friends that, at least.

"Last wishes?" The corner of Ed's mouth quirked up. "What's that? Like a last meal?"

"It's what we do when we Wake people," I said. "Ask if they have a last wish we can help fulfill, like sending a message to loved ones."

"Don't have any loved ones left." Ed shrugged.

"It doesn't have to be a message," I said. "It can be anything you need help with that's unfinished . . ." I trailed off, giving them time to think, hoping for something that would make this less awful.

Tamsin cleared her throat. "I'm, uh—I'm going to gather my supplies and get ready while you do this," she said, picking her bag up and backing away from the table before halting. "Oh. Hair, please."

I pulled a few strands out and passed them over to her.

"See you down there." She dashed off, leaving the rest of us standing awkwardly around the table. A few silent minutes passed.

"I don't have anyone to spread my ashes," Ed said suddenly.

"Good!" I exclaimed, desperately glad to have something to grab on to. Then I caught the wide-eyed looks everyone was giving me and realized how that had sounded. "Not *good*—I mean we can help with that? If you want?"

"I think if you folks wouldn't mind spreading them along the trail in the park," Ed said. "I'd like that. Let me enjoy the sunshine."

"Okay," I said, taking a deep breath. That was one. "Yeah. We can do that, Ed."

He gave me a short nod and a little wink before heading downstairs with Alex.

"Last wish," Paulette said to herself, pursing her lips. "Hm. I'd ask you to finish my novel for me, but I don't know that anyone else could do justice to my vision."

Please have another option, I silently begged. Something I *could* do justice to.

"Oh." She broke into a small, pleased smile. "I've got it," she said. "How about planting a tree in your backyard so you can go sit under it and read and think of me?"

That sounded possible, but I looked to Mom for confirmation.

"That's a lovely idea, Paulette," Mom said. "We can absolutely do that."

"Good!" Paulette beamed, clasping her hands together. "That's good." Her smile dimmed a bit as she nodded to herself. "I'll head down, then."

Mom and I turned to Devon as she left. He was staring resolutely down at the table.

"I'd like to tell mine to Kimmy in private," he said.

She frowned at that and began shaking her head. "We need to get this spell done—"

"Mom!" I hurried around to her side of the table. "We can still take the time to do this," I began and she grabbed my arm, cutting me off.

"You have no way of knowing that," she said. "We have no idea what this is doing to you and how long you actually have and I *refuse* to waste any more time—"

"It's not a waste," I said. "We owe them all this much. It's my time to give and it's worth it to spend it on this."

An entire spectrum of emotions crossed over Mom's face before she finally stepped away. "Don't take too long," she said as she headed for the prep room. "Please."

Devon and I stood quietly as I gave him space. This was his last wish. I wasn't about to rush him, no matter how Mom felt about it.

"I want you to make sure the memory spell stays on my family," he blurted out suddenly.

"What?" Of all the things—

"I think it's better that way." He poked at a stain on the table, not meeting my eyes.

"Devon." It might be *his* last wish, but I didn't think he knew what he was asking.

"I don't want them to have to live with this," Devon said, finally looking up. "It wouldn't be happening if I hadn't snuck out. I can't leave knowing how sad they'd be. Don't let them be sad, okay?" He swiped at his cheeks before clearing his throat. "Besides, you'll remember me. Make that another promise."

"That's two last wishes." I sniffed.

"I could keep going," he offered with a crooked grin. "Portrait of me in the front foyer. Maybe another tree beside Paulette's so you can put a hammock up. Gimme a few more minutes. I can come up with more."

"And I'll start a list," I said.

"Kids." Mom stood near the top of the stairs. "Everything okay up here?"

"Yes, ma'am," Devon said, heading toward her. "We were on our way down."

No more stalling.

It was time.

Everyone was set up downstairs.

Ed and Paulette were sitting on their tables and a small gurney had been pulled out for Devon. Alex and Tamsin were off to the side and a circle of grey powder filled up the center of the room. Four rocks with designs painted on them were set around the circle. A line of smaller stones led out from the painted stone closest to Tamsin and a crystal sat at the end of it.

Devon joined Ed and Paulette while Mom came over to wrap an arm around my shoulders.

"Okay," Tamsin said, knitting her fingers together nervously. "Now you go stand inside the circle."

"And then what?" I asked, eyeing the whole setup.

"Then I activate the spell and fingers crossed it works."

Mom prodded me and I stepped inside the circle. I couldn't look at the three behind me. I'd leap back out again. *This is for the best*, I reminded myself.

TUG. TUG. TUG.

I'm sorry.

Mom was right. Being alive was more important. I could still help Tamsin come up with a plan to use this spell on the witch next. I could fulfill Ed, Paulette, and Devon's last wishes.

I didn't need the power to do any of that.

And yet—everything about this screamed *wrong*.

TUG. TUG. TUG.

I had the strangest urge to see if the power had a last wish.

"Ready?" Tamsin whispered to me, and I shook my head. "On three," she said.

I took a deep breath.

"Three," Tamsin called out, raising her foot and stomping it down on the crystal. A blast of light traveled up the line of stones before hitting the painted rock and the entire circle around me exploded in a wave of energy.

I woke up on the floor.

Mom, Alex, and Tamsin were also on the floor, blinking slowly as they tried to sit up.

My ears were ringing.

I patted myself down, making sure I was all in one piece and pleasantly surprised to find I was. What about everyone else, though? "Is everyone okay?"

"Well," Ed's gravelly voice said, "I'm not dead yet."

Chapter Twenty-Three

That was bad.

But good, too? Ed, Paulette, and Devon were still here. Moaning, but alive.

It was mostly bad, though. Probably.

My head hurt too much to figure out where to land on the whole thing.

"Tamsin," Mom gritted out as she staggered to her feet. "What happened?"

"Backlash." Tamsin groaned.

"So, it didn't work." I flopped back on the floor. Now what?

"It didn't just not work." She shuffled over to sit closer, examining me. "Something in you *repelled* the spell."

Six pairs of eyes locked on to me.

"Not on purpose!" I exclaimed.

"What do we do now?" Devon asked as he slid off the tray.

"I'll see if I can detect a cause, but . . ." Tamsin trailed off with an apologetic shrug.

"We need to be prepared in case you can't," Alex said. "What do you think?" He looked over at Mom and she pressed her lips together before huffing out a breath.

"That's our best bet," she said. "I'll stay down here with Tamsin and Kimmy if the rest of you can work on identifying the witch."

"We're on it," Paulette declared, waving a finger in the air and leading the way upstairs. "Come on, boys. Back to the murder board!"

Ed and Devon fell into line behind her while Alex brought up the rear. Mom caught his eye before he left and mouthed "good luck." He flashed a little heart with his fingers in return.

Then Mom, Tamsin, and I were left, surrounded by crystal shards, painted rocks, and a cloud of uncertainty.

"I wish we had our own whiteboard," Tamsin said, breaking through the silence. She clapped her hands together. "Possible reasons why the spell was repelled. I think option number one is that the wild magic of your power is lashing out. Your aura—" She waved a hand in a loose circle in front of me. "It's distinctly brighter and starting to spike a bit."

That didn't sound like an option with a solution.

"What else could it be?" Mom came down to sit beside me, wrapping an arm around my shoulders.

Tug, tug, tug.

I grimaced a little, rubbing a fist against the phantom ache the tugs left in my chest. Mom jumped right on me for it.

"What's wrong? I thought you weren't hurt. Did the spell do something?"

"No." I waved her off. "Remember how I told you I get those tugs sometimes now? From the power?"

Mom whipped her head up to Tamsin. "Is that the wild magic? Could it be damaging her heart?"

Tamsin sat down cross-legged in front of us, a small frown on her face. "You mentioned these tugs before. When did they start exactly? Describe them?"

"After Grandma died," I said. "That was when I first noticed the power getting stronger—even before I broke the cap. The power was always more of a vibration before, but then all of a sudden, it was these tugs. Right here." I pointed to the spot. "Really insistent and intense sometimes. I don't know how else to describe it."

"Hmm." Tamsin hummed to herself, eyeing me carefully. "Let's try something. Sit like this with your hands on your knees and close your eyes."

I had no idea where she was going with this, but I was on board for anything that might get us answers. In position, I waited. "Now what?"

"Breathe and reach for your power," she said, voice calm and even. "Seek out the open connections you have."

Taking a few centering breaths, I focused, reaching for that connection to my power within myself.

"Tell me who you find," Tamsin whispered.

Deep breath in. Sending the power out. Searching. Finding the connections.

"Devon," I said, recognizing the first one and then seeking out the rest. "Ed. Paulette."

And—

"Kimmy?" Tamsin prompted.

"Grandma," I admitted. "But I always do. It's a leftover of the family connection, right? Like an echo or something? It's not really there."

Not anymore.

"See where it leads. Please."

I found the faint connection again and pulsed my power into it, exploring the shape of it. It was a small thread, like the one I used to feel when I was training with her.

I followed it. Twisting back around deep, deep into the center of my power.

There at the core.

A spark.

I held my breath

"Grandma?"

Tug, tug, tug.

"*Bev?*" Mom stared incredulously between me and Tamsin. "How—I don't understand. What's happening?"

"My best guess is that during the attack, Bev was able to use their connection to send her spark to Kimmy before the witch could capture it all," Tamsin said. She turned to me, regret filling her face. "We didn't meet until after that, so I didn't clock it as a change to your power."

"It's not your fault," I said faintly, trying to wrap my brain around this.

Grandma had been here with me the whole time.

Chapter Twenty-Four

"**W**hat does this mean for Kimmy?" Mom asked, but I was still stuck on *Grandma's spark is inside me.*

Five months of missing her, of being so mad that she'd had no unfinished business, and she'd been right here. I hadn't found her spark before because I'd been looking inside her instead of inside myself.

Why? Was it to try and escape the witch? Or was she trying to help me somehow? Is this why I was able to Wake Devon—

"That's why I could break the cap," I gasped. All of the pieces were falling into place. "Because of the extra boost from Grandma."

Which led to the wild magic and everything that had followed.

But Grandma had been scared of testing the limits of our power. Scared enough to hide it from me for a long time. Mom started throwing question after question at Tamsin, who tried her best to keep up, but I didn't see the point. We should be asking the person who had the actual answers.

Except she couldn't talk.

Grandma?

TUG, TUG, TUG.

I guess she could still communicate in her own way. Which was good because I had plenty of questions of my own.

Why did you want me to Wake Devon?

Why did you help me break the cap?

Why didn't you tell me about the cost?

Why won't you talk to me?

No tugs.

No answers.

Nothing.

I shoved down my frustration and tuned back in to Mom and Tamsin's conversation.

"My spell was specifically targeted for Kimmy," Tamsin said. "But Bev's presence in Kimmy is active enough to disrupt it. I think we need to return to the previous plan of trying the spell on the witch."

"What if there's a trace of Bev left in the witch?" Mom asked.

"I factored that into my calculations." Tamsin nodded. "Based on how frequently she attacks, she absorbs the energy from her victims quickly and this many months later, um . . . it wouldn't be an issue."

Meaning any part of Grandma that the witch had managed to get was gone for sure.

I had the only part left.

"But there's still a chance she's too strong," Mom pressed. "Even if we track her down and trap her and use this spell, you can't guarantee it won't backfire."

An idea started to form in my brain and before I could dismiss it—

Tug, tug, tug.

I mentally rolled my eyes. *Now you're talking to me? Is this you letting me know I'm on to something?*

Tug, tug, tug.

"What would it take?" I asked Tamsin, rolling with Grandma's possible encouragement. "To make sure it worked?"

"Strip out every stolen bit of life force she has? That would weaken her." Tamsin dragged a hand through her hair and grimaced. "It's not exactly something we can work out with trial and error. We get one shot."

Steal back the stolen sparks. I'd already managed to do that with Devon, Ed, and Paulette. If I was close enough, if I could touch her? I might be able to get the rest.

I shuddered. It was dangerous and probably not smart at all *and* had a decent chance of failing, but I couldn't see any better options for us. "I think I can do that," I said.

Mom and Tamsin stared at me, wide-eyed.

"Tell me *exactly* what's going through your brain right now," Mom said.

"My power is getting stronger—and I *know* that's ultimately a bad thing, but what if we took advantage of it while we can?" With the wild magic, I was the only one who could match forces with the witch. "I think I could connect to any sparks she still has and pull them out."

"Weakening her for the spell," Tamsin said. "That could work."

"If we could surprise her and trap her somewhere," I said. "I could sneak in and take the sparks and then you could use your spell."

"I'm not agreeing to this," Mom said. "But how do you suggest trapping her?"

"I could use the Bomb Be Gone ingredients," Tamsin said suddenly. "We could use the powders to circle her and contain her negative energy. You and Alex could help spread it while—"

"You think she'll walk into a trap so easily?" Mom wasn't going to get onboard with this plan without a fight.

"She wants the sparks back," I said. "If we had Devon, Ed, and Paulette—"

"What?" Mom's jaw dropped. "As bait?"

"We have no other way to fix this," I said. "If we put her focus on them, she'll be distracted and the rest of the plan can fall into place. Once it works, her hold would be *gone*. We'll put the cap back on me, I'll release everyone, and they can pass on," I said.

All of the stolen sparks. Including Devon, Ed, and Paulette.

And Grandma.

"Danger and recklessness aside . . . ," Mom threw her hands up. "How do you plan to do this when we have no idea who she is?"

The door at the top of the stairs crashed open, hitting the wall and we all jumped.

"We figured out who the witch is!" Devon bellowed.

Mom muttered something under her breath before

gathering herself. "Thank you, Devon," she called, flinching as the door slammed again. She sighed. "Shall we?"

The three of us stood up and headed for the stairs.

Mom stared at the murder board in dismay.

"Dr. Vernon's niece?" she cried. "But she's so nice."

"I mean . . ." I pointed at our three recently deceased guests. "Clearly not."

"How did you put it together?" Tamsin asked as she took in the scribbled notes all over the board.

"The death certificates," Paulette said proudly, twirling a marker in her fingers. "We didn't have facts about the witch herself so we started looking at her victims."

"Aside from Devon," Alex said, "everyone on our suspected victim list died of 'natural causes.'"

"Which was a bunch of hooey because I was healthy as a horse," Ed said. "You get to a certain age and it's easy for people to write it off as your time to go."

"After that insight from Ed," Alex continued, "we looked at the death certificates and realized they all had the same signature."

"Dr. Chloe Wardwell," Devon announced as Paulette circled the name with a flourish.

"I knew her voice was familiar," Alex said, tapping a

finger against his temple. "Hearing it come out of Devon threw me off and I couldn't place it."

"It's the perfect cover," Mom said before gasping. "She must have killed Dr. Vernon, too. Taking over his practice gave her the coroner role, easy access to the hospital, visits to the long-term care homes, everything! No one would've questioned it."

"She only had to murder her own uncle to do it," Ed said, crossing his arms and leaning back in his chair with disgust.

"You guys—" Tamsin looked around the room at everyone. "You know that's a spell, right? There's no way he's her uncle."

"Another memory spell?"

Tamsin shook her head at my question. "Maybe, but it could also be a suggestion plant," she said. "She tells the story to a few key people and uses the magic to sell it, but then they tell other people which spreads the story organically and the more it spreads, the stronger it grows. She doesn't have to lift a finger."

I looked over the notes on the board.

This wasn't sitting right for me.

"She goes to the trouble of setting up a cover job so she can falsify death certificates and cover her tracks," I said.

"That says she's careful. She plans."

"It helped her pick her victims too," Alex said. "Very methodical."

"Right." I pointed at him before tapping Devon's name on the board. And Grandma's. "But then she also took risks," I said. "She took Grandma outside the grocery store and Devon in the park, risking witnesses for the sake of an extra power boost."

"Opportunistic and she was lucky not to get caught," Tamsin said. "Plus, she had her work cut out for her to cover up her tracks with Devon."

"When I went to find him at the morgue," I said, "she was about to head in, but got called away. She didn't try to avoid the page so she wasn't worried about leaving him."

"She's overconfident," Alex said, borrowing the marker from Paulette to start making notes under Dr. Wardwell's name on the board.

"No one's stopped her for more than a hundred years so why would anything get in the way now?" Tamsin agreed. "Arrogance is feeding the impulsiveness."

Paulette narrowed her eyes at the board, taking it all in. "How can we use all of that to our advantage?"

Quiet filled the kitchen as everyone deliberated on that.

I knew how we could use that to our advantage, but I'd already put my idea out there. Someone else had to come up with one.

Or agree to mine.

"We surprise her," Mom finally said. "She doesn't know that we know who she is and . . . she doesn't know what Kimmy's capable of."

I couldn't be hearing this correctly. "You're going to let me try?"

"You were right," she said. "We need to use our advantages while we have them."

"Try what?" Devon asked.

"Something I'm going to need your help with," I said. "You and Ed and Paulette." This wasn't a move I wanted to make without their consent. It was our best chance. Probably our only chance. But I wasn't forging ahead again without their permission.

I outlined the plan that we'd discussed downstairs.

"I meant what I said." Paulette smiled softly at me. "I don't want her to harm anyone else. I'm in."

"Same here, kid," Ed agreed.

Making myself look at Devon, I tried to brace for what I'd find.

"Told you. I know how this ends," he said, giving me

a little shrug. "Might as well get to see you use your cool superpowers again on the way."

"It's like we're in *Lord of the Rings*," Paulette whispered. She turned to me solemnly. "You have my sword."

"And my bow," Alex added, making her break into another grin.

"I'm sorry," Devon said, putting up a hand. "We've had access to weapons *this whole time*?"

"It's from a movie, kid," Ed said. "You're supposed to say 'and my axe.'"

"I can have an *axe*?"

"No! There's no—" I gave up trying to explain. "Can we get back to the plan?"

Everyone burst into a flurry of activity. Mom, Alex, and Paulette huddled at the board, trying to work out the best spot for an ambush. Tamsin recruited the rest of us to help put together modified Be Gone Bomb powder while she organized her supplies for the spell.

"Do these still need the pepper?" Devon sneezed as he poured it into a bowl.

"Ooh, not that much," Tamsin said, reaching over to help.

There was a knock at the front door and Alex popped his head out of their huddle. "I locked it," he said. "I didn't want anyone walking in while we were . . ." He gestured at the board.

The knock sounded again. Louder.

"They'll leave when we don't answer," Mom said, waving it off.

Then we heard the front door open.

"I locked it," Alex said again, eyes wide.

Tamsin got up first, motioning for us to stay back, but we all followed her out into the hallway.

Dr. Wardwell stood in the front foyer, kicking the door shut behind her. "I *did* knock."

Chapter Twenty-Five

Dr. Wardwell looked so *normal*, standing there in the middle of the foyer like she was dropping by for a casual visit. Her blond hair was tied back in a twisty bun and she was still in her scrubs. She wore a pair of beat-up running shoes that squeaked with each step.

But red lips against pale skin showed the truth as they curled up into a sharp smile.

"How did she get in?" Mom whispered to me and Tamsin. "I thought the house was protected?"

"And I *locked* the door," Alex added.

"Unlocking a door is nothing," Dr. Wardwell said, trailing a finger along the leaves of the lilies by the front door. "And your protections need to be refreshed, because breaking them was far too easy."

I caught Tamsin's gaze and saw the same panic crawling up my throat reflected there. She didn't have her spell together yet. We had no defenses.

All we had was me.

"I'll try and hold her off," I murmured. "Get the things you need for the spell."

If I could start siphoning the life forces out of her, maybe Tamsin could be ready fast enough to swoop in—

"Ah, ah, ah," Dr. Wardwell said. She shook her head at Tamsin, who was sneaking toward the kitchen. "I need everyone together for this."

Devon, Ed, and Paulette turned as one. Eyes glowing bright blue.

Devon grabbed on to Tamsin, Ed on to Alex, and Paulette on to Mom, their faces going slack as Dr. Wardwell started to drain them.

"You can't blame me for dropping in like this," Dr. Wardwell said. "Not when you kept stealing from me."

I had to stop this. I had to pull them back. I had to—

I had to try.

Focusing with everything I had, I sent the power out to search for whatever life forces were trapped inside the witch. My hands glowed and the golden light arced through the air in one solid beam, hitting Dr. Wardwell dead center.

She grunted in shock.

It was working. I stretched the power as far as I could, catching hints of the energies at the edge of my senses, but they kept slipping out of my reach.

My hands shook.

Grandma. Help.

Something stirred, but it wasn't Grandma.

"I've lived for years off the dim remains of dying sparks," Dr. Wardwell said, rallying. "Yours is so *rich* and bright."

The force of her power met mine head on—not to push me back.

Pulling me in.

"I promise to savor it," she said.

I tried to fight her, but I couldn't keep a grasp on the power. Couldn't stop the flow as it rushed out of me. My limbs were getting heavy.

I couldn't stop her.

I—

Tug, tug, tug.

It took a moment for the sensation to register.

I don't think you can help me now, Grandma. This is too much. I can't fight her.

Tug, tug, TUG.

You think I should fight?

Silence.

My legs went out and I fell to the floor.

You think I should let go?

TUG, TUG, TUG.

Why would she tell me that? Why wouldn't she just *help* me?

Tug, tug, tug.

Even when it was hard to trust myself, I'd always trusted Grandma. There were secrets and hurt and *death* between us now, but I decided to trust her again.

One last time.

I let Dr. Wardwell pull me in.

Everything went dark.

Time stretched.

I was in another space. The between place inside Dr. Wardwell where instead of her own vibrant life force, there was a dragon's hoard of fragmented, torn pieces of the lives of others.

It was an odd sensation. I was me, but not me. Not in any form I recognized. Pure energy. Not seeing or speaking, but sensing everything around me.

Like the familiar presence at my side.

Grandma.

She moved in close and instead of tugs, this time it was flashes of images.

Dr. Wardwell approaching Grandma while she was sitting in her car.

Reaching through the window.

Draining the life out of her with no one around to stop it.

Thinking of me.

Desperately trying to stay. Grabbing on to our connection. Following it.

Finding a piece of herself back with me.

Communicating the only way she could.

Watching as the witch consumed more people and trying to nudge me in the right direction. Seeing it all spiral. Believing I could stop it.

Being here with me now.

Ready to help.

Help how? What could I do with no body and no clue? Grandma nudged me and I realized we had company. Ed. Paulette. Devon. Tamsin. Alex. And Mom.

Dr. Wardwell got us all in the end.

Grandma nudged me again. Harder this time.

Another flash.

The golden light of our power surrounding Dr. Wardwell's core of stolen energy and ripping it away.

Would that—would that work? Did our power still exist in here?

Grandma nudged everyone, urging us all forward, until we were up close and personal with the witch's stash. There were *dozens* of sparks.

I would never have been able to do this on my own.

Grandma started to whirl around the core and Tamsin followed her. The rest of us joined in, completing the circle. We were a golden glow spinning around the fragmented life forces, warming them up, sharing our energy, connecting with them in a web of power.

A flash from Grandma to—

PULL

—as hard as we could.

The witch screamed—a cry that echoed through this space and beyond. Everything fractured around us—

And then I opened my eyes, back in my body and on the floor. Again. I looked up in time to see Dr. Wardwell turn to dust with nothing of her own left to sustain her.

Tamsin was going to be sad she didn't get to use her spell.

I struggled to my feet and tried to blink the spots out of

my eyes when I realized they were sparks. All of the sparks we'd pulled out of Dr. Wardwell, floating around me like fireflies.

Six of them, I recognized—three full and three not-quite-full—and sent them back where they belonged. I couldn't help the relieved laugh at the groans and moans of my family and friends as they started to come to.

The rest of the sparks hovered in the air above me. The last energy of people the witch had killed—no longer tethered here, bodies long gone. Waiting to be at rest.

Would they be stuck here until we put the cap on and my wild magic was under control again? I tested the hold my power had on them and was shocked at how it loosened.

Tamsin said—

Oh. Of course. She said the wild magic was driven to seek out and heal. The only way to help these sparks finish healing was to let them pass over to wherever they were meant to be.

I released them and one by one, they faded away until there was only one remaining. It floated in front of me for a moment before disappearing into my chest.

Tug, tug, tug.

My breath caught.

Grandma.

Chapter Twenty-Six

Grandma was still here. She hadn't left.

I'm sorry.

I sent the words at her desperately, hoping she understood. I should have said them earlier, but everything had been moving so quickly.

I'm sorry for every angry thought I had because I was so sure you left me behind.

I didn't mean it.

I waited, every second stretching out longer than the last until—

Tug, tug, tug.

A rush of relief flooded through me and I pressed a hand against my heart.

Thank you.

There was rustling around as everyone was finally fully conscious, standing, and patting themselves down to make sure they were in one piece.

"Kimmy?" Mom came over and rested a hand on my cheek. "Are you okay, sweetheart? You're as white as a sheet."

"I'm fine, I'm just—" I rubbed at my chest. "Talking to Grandma."

"She's still here?" Mom's eyebrows shot up and she leaned in close. "Hello, Bev," she said loudly, and I flapped a hand at her.

"Stop," I said. "I don't think that makes a difference. Talk normal, please."

"Hi, Bev," Alex said with a grin.

Tug, tug, tug.

I was almost afraid to ask, but I had to know. *What is this? Do I get to keep you here? Forever?*

No answer.

Bits of the conversation between the adults floated over to me. They were talking about how soon the cap could be put back in place. Did we really have to jump on that immediately? We couldn't let everyone take a minute?

Devon wandered over to stand beside me. "I guess it's

time to say goodbye for real," he said.

My heart dropped at the thought of going downstairs again and saying goodbye again and letting go *again*.

Tug, tug, tug.

I closed my eyes.

"Kimmy?" Devon whispered.

"Give me a minute," I whispered back.

What are you trying to tell me?

An image flashed through my brain, like before. When we were in the other place.

The cracked sparks of Devon, Ed, and Paulette. Not whole, but not completely broken.

My power was currently filling in those cracks and keeping them alive. Grandma sent me another flash with a plan for a permanent fix: use her spark to repair the other three.

No!

I flinched back and Devon touched my shoulder gently. "Are you okay? You're shaking." He guided me over until I was sitting down in one of the chairs against the wall. The conversation between Tamsin and the others stopped, but their questions turned to white noise.

All I could focus on was Grandma. Her and her *awful* plan. It wasn't that I didn't want to save the others.

But she was asking me to go through losing her a second time.

I just got you back. Stop leaving me.

A rapid series of flashes from her then, one after the other: *Grandma and me making cookies, Grandma training me down in the prep room and giving me a pat, pat, pat on my shoulder after a job well done, her and me laughing as we worked in the garden, Grandma and Mom teaching me how to ride a bike, the two of us in the kitchen with Alex making dinner together, and more. On and on.*

Our lifetime of memories together.

Memories weren't the same as having her with me.

More flashes: *me lecturing Mom on the cookie table, me showing Tamsin how to set up the flowers, me typing up a last-wish letter, me scolding Devon on his table manners.*

The message was clear. She was always going to be with me in some way.

I blinked away tears.

We still should have had more time. How could she ask me to do this?

A single image showed up crystal clear in my mind. Her typewriter with the special paper beside it. This was a last wish. The rule was we always did our best to honor them and she knew I couldn't argue with that.

"Okay," I whispered, reaching for the power. "Okay, Grandma."

Tug, tug, tug.

I let the tears fall. *I love you, too.*

Grandma's spark vibrated in my chest as it split into three. Taking a deep breath, I sent each glowing piece through the connections to Ed, Paulette, and Devon.

"What's happening?" Devon whispered.

"Hold still," I said. In my mind's eye, I could see the three fragments colliding with their damaged sparks. Golden light spread through the cracks, filling them in until every fracture was healed. My connection to each of them glowed bright and then snapped.

Ed, Paulette, and Devon gasped as the last light of Grandma faded away.

"I don't understand," Paulette said, pressing a hand against her chest. "Was that—"

"Grandma." I nodded. "She fixed the damage with her spark. It's what she wanted."

"We're not going to die?" Devon asked tentatively.

"Not right now," I said. "Hopefully not for a while."

Ed nodded, taking a shaky breath. "Well, that is a gift. Thank you, Bev."

"What about the connection? The drain on you?" Alex

asked as he and Mom rushed over to me and understanding bloomed on Tamsin's face.

"The wild magic recognized that they were healed," she said. "It released them on its own."

Mom grabbed me, wrapping me up in a hug. Tears trickled down on to the top of my head as she squeezed me tight. Alex embraced us both from the other side and then, one by one, I found myself in the middle of a giant group hug.

Devon's muffled voice managed to make its way through the huddle. "Am I allowed to go home now?"

Epilogue

Two weeks later, everything was quiet.

Mostly because I was *incredibly* grounded.

There had been a flurry of activity after the group hug broke up. The memory spell surrounding Devon ended with the witch's death and Alex took him home immediately so his family wouldn't have a chance to notice he was missing.

For Ed and Paulette, however, we needed two fresh memory spells to cover things up so they'd be free to rejoin the land of the living. Tamsin ended up calling her mom for help which meant she'd had to confess everything she'd been up to. That was a lively conversation.

The important thing was the spells worked and Ed and Paulette were able to go home.

They came back the next day.

And the next. And the one after that. They'd bring books, help with the garden, and stay for dinner more often than not. Mom and Alex finally gave them both part-time jobs.

We needed the help since Tamsin left. Temporarily.

Her family had arrived the day after we defeated the witch and helped her place the cap back on my power. She had a long talk with them while they were here. She wanted to stick around and help me learn more about magic and they wanted her to finish school.

They compromised and she was transferring to a college close by . . .

To get her mortuary science degree! She came by for dinner more often than not as well and it was nice. I liked having more people around.

I hadn't seen Devon since he went home.

I understood.

I did.

I didn't want to bother him while he was readjusting, either. Mom said wait and see so that's what I was doing. That plus a million chores since I was so very grounded.

"Kimmy!" Mom hollered up the stairs. "Have you finished yet?"

"No!" I yelled back. "Soon!"

I was clearing space to set up the last-wish desk in my room. The rearranging was done and now I was ready to grab everything from Grandma's room.

Scooting across the hall, I opened the door and stepped inside. We'd tidied up after the mess with the journals and now Mom and I were talking about starting to sort through Grandma's things. Moving the last-wish stuff was the first step.

It would be nice to have it in my room, even if I wasn't going to be using it exactly how Grandma had intended.

I was taking a break from using the power.

Mom, Alex, and I had talked it over from top to bottom. When they first suggested it, I immediately said no. I couldn't even think about it. Using the power was my link to Dad and Grandma. But then I slowly remembered: it wasn't my only link.

The biggest concern Mom and Alex had was the whole waking-people-at-the-expense-of-my-own-life-force thing. Mom's point was that every minute was valuable when none of us knew how long we had. I could understand that.

I'd take more minutes with Dad and Grandma if I could.

And yet—

Even if it meant using up my time, Waking people and honoring last wishes still felt like a worthy cause.

Mom wasn't asking me to quit, though. Just take a break and really think about what it meant to give people that gift. Alex said it was a decision worth giving space to.

In the meantime, Tamsin was going to teach me about other methods of magic and maybe, someday, I'd be able to Wake people in a safer way. Dad would be pretty proud if we could pull that off, I thought.

Alex had also brought up an idea. A lovely one. He suggested we incorporate the last wishes into our regular funeral planning services. Offer people the chance to leave a note or a final gift that could be delivered after their services were over. Mom and I were working together on a little brochure to add to our packages.

Maybe people would take us up on it, maybe they wouldn't. If even one person did, I'd be happy. It was a different way to keep the tradition alive and made it something the three of us could do together. I wasn't sure what Grandma would have thought of that, but I hoped she'd be happy, too.

Heading over to the little desk, I picked up the typewriter. A piece of paper fluttered to the floor. An envelope, actually. With my name on it.

I picked it up carefully, recognizing Grandma's handwriting.

Was this a last-wish letter? We'd completed a last wish for her when she saved the others, but this was—she'd taken the time to type this out at some point. *Months* ago, maybe longer.

Why? Just in case I couldn't Wake her? I would have if it hadn't been for Dr. Wardwell stealing her spark. Was this her last wish as it would have been? Before everything happened?

Whatever it was, it was a goodbye.

My last one from Grandma.

Just *open it*, Kimmy.

Taking a deep breath, I opened the envelope. There was a letter and a piece of cardstock inside. I set down the cardstock and the envelope to read the letter first.

Dear Kimmy,

Your father passed away this week.

Wait, what? Dad died ten years ago. She wrote this back then and kept it that long? I didn't know what to think about that.

It was unexpected and as much as I hope that you and I will have many years together, it reminded me that time is never guaranteed for anyone. I wanted to make sure you had this.

Just in case.

With so much love,

Grandma Bev

That was it. The whole letter.

So, what did she want me to have?

I picked up the small rectangular piece of cardstock. A sweet smell wafted off of it, instantly transporting me to sunny afternoons in the kitchen with Grandma. The card was covered in carefully typed words and messily handwritten notes with the title clear at the top.

Bev's Cookies

Her top-secret cookie recipe that she never shared with anyone. Tears welled up as I traced a finger over her notes written in the margins of the recipe. Corrections on the amount of vanilla extract. A scribble of "people in this family like them crispy!" along the bottom. It was a little thing, but an important thing. Another piece of Grandma to keep with me.

I leapt up from my bed and ran downstairs. "Mom!

You'll never guess what I found!" I nearly tripped over Morris on the bottom step when someone knocked at the front door.

Standing there was my second surprise of the day—Devon.

He shuffled his feet on the porch, looking around nervously and biting at his lip.

"Hi!" I said, smiling brightly and opening the door wider. I didn't want him to be *nervous*. Not here. Even if it was a place full of unpleasant memories for him.

I really hoped I wasn't one of them.

"Is this a bad time?" Devon asked.

"No," I said. "Come on in. What's up?"

"I'm sorry I didn't come by earlier," Devon said, stepping inside hesitantly. "I kind of wanted to forget about everything for a while."

I couldn't blame him for that.

"But then, I don't know," he said, scratching at the back of his neck. "I also missed you? And thought maybe you'd want to hang out?" He gave me a look. "Wait, do you hang out with regular people or is it strictly not-dead dead people?"

"Oh, wow," I said. "I didn't miss you *at all*."

"That's a yes." Devon cracked a grin and bumped

his shoulder against mine. "Want to go for a bike ride or something?"

I grimaced. "My bike privileges have been revoked for another two weeks," I said. "Grounded for the whole sneaking-out-of-the-house-and-into-the-morgue-to-Wake-you thing."

"Ah," Devon said, scrunching up his face in sympathy. "That sucks. Maybe—"

"Devon!" Mom headed down the hall toward us. "I thought I heard your voice. It's nice to see you. How have you been?"

"Good," he said. "Yeah, I'm good. I came by to see if Kimmy was free—"

"Don't worry." I sighed. "I told him I'm grounded."

"I think we can make an exception for today," Mom said. "As long as you stay here." She patted Devon's shoulder and wandered off into her office.

"An exception," Devon said, raising his eyebrows at me. "I feel special."

"Come on." I grabbed his arm and started dragging him toward the kitchen. "We'll see how special you feel after I put you to work. How are you at making cookies?"

I had some unfinished business to take care of.

BEV'S COOKIES

Ingredients

1 ¼ cups all-purpose flour

½ teaspoon baking soda

room temp → ½ cup butter → salted! v. important

¼ cup sugar

do not try and reduce ½ cup packed brown sugar

1 egg

more like 2 1 ½ teaspoon vanilla → let it spill over a bit as you measure

1 cup semisweet chocolate chips chunk

enough to well populate the dough

+ butterscotch chips +caramel bits +dark chocolate chips

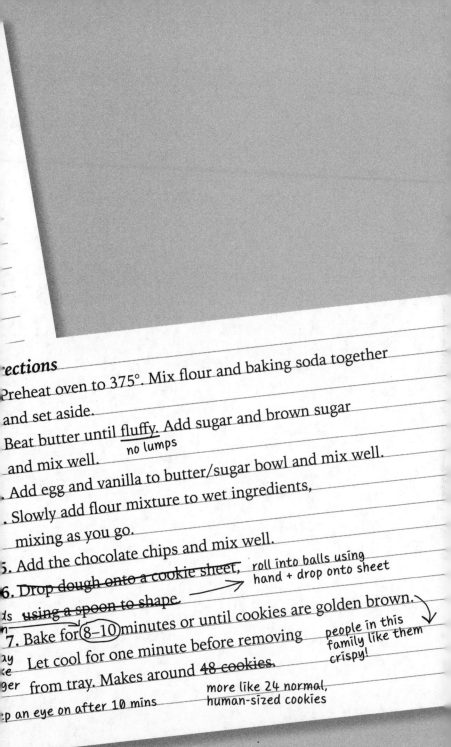

ections

Preheat oven to 375°. Mix flour and baking soda together and set aside.

Beat butter until fluffy. Add sugar and brown sugar and mix well. ~no lumps~

. Add egg and vanilla to butter/sugar bowl and mix well.

. Slowly add flour mixture to wet ingredients, mixing as you go.

5. Add the chocolate chips and mix well.

6. ~~Drop dough onto a cookie sheet,~~ roll into balls using hand + drop onto sheet

~ds~ ~~using a spoon to shape.~~

~n~

7. Bake for (8–10) minutes or until cookies are golden brown.

~y~ Let cool for one minute before removing people in this family like them

~ke~ from tray. Makes around ~~48 cookies.~~ crispy!

~ger~ more like 24 normal, human-sized cookies

~p an eye on after 10 mins~

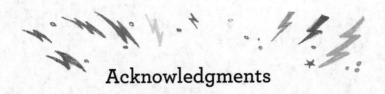

Acknowledgments

Thank you to my editor, Martha Mihalick, for your endless patience and encouragement on this particular story adventure. And a warm thank-you to the rest of the Greenwillow and HarperCollins teams, including Virginia Duncan, Arianna Robinson, Tim Smith, Sylvie Le Floc'h, Robby Imfeld, Samantha Brown, and the incredible folks of the marketing, publicity, and sales departments.

To my agent, Molly Ker Hawn, thank you for always being an oasis of calm when I am . . . not. I appreciate you!

Thank you to Andy Smith for another incredible cover.

To Janet Johnson, Laura Shovan, Rebecca Donnelly, and Timanda Wertz, thank you for your encouragement when this idea was more enthusiasm than actual written words. And to Margaret Dilloway, thank you for being a speed reader and giving me notes when this was still the draftiest of first drafts.

Thank you to Bill Denning and Mary-Lyn Denning for kindly sharing your knowledge of and personal experience with funeral homes. I greatly appreciated it. (Any inaccuracies are of my own doing and for plot purposes!)

To Zoë Reilly-Ansons and the team at the Middlesex County Library: thank you for your continuous support.

Thank you to my friends and family who amiably wait for me to socialize between deadlines. And the ultimate thank-you to my mom and dad, who have read every draft and helped bounce every idea. I love you all very much.